Satan's Diary

Steven Darrell Bates

Edited by: M.D. DeCillis & Dianne Giambusso

Publisher Name: Steven & Tulane Bates

ISBN #: 978-1-7352227-0-7

I dedicate this book to my wife Tulane- it's a privilege
to share my business, life, and love with you.

To my children Steven Jr. and Sarah – your growth
provides a constant source of joy and pride.

To everyone who helped me achieve my
dream. Thank you so much!!!

Steven Darrell Bates

Contents

I walked into my bedroom and tossed my black, carry-on bag on the bed. I was tired from working excessive hours, and the relatively short flight from Cincinnati to Atlanta seemed unusually long. I just wanted to melt away my frustration with a warm bath and relax for the rest of the evening. A project I was working on had failed miserably, but in my line of business, I have learned that it's almost inevitable that some things don't go according to plan.

I grabbed the remote control and turned on the TV, my favorite form of relaxation. Unfortunately, surfing channels gave me no such peace today. Surfing the dozens of channels accentuated the mistakes I had made during my project.

I kept switching channels without thinking until I came to a familiar face on BET. The comical young Elvis hairstyle and poorly made makeup couldn't conceal the familiar face of Peter Popoff.

I smirked to myself and shook my head. Out of all the infomercials and weird people on late-night TV, I landed on old double P.

I swear this guy is like the terminator; he just keeps coming back!

Peter got my attention in the late '70s. I had heard whispers about Popoff misleading his small flock of worshipers, but that was nothing new. Church leaders had been misleading people for years.

What I thought was unique about his followers was, not only were his followers willing to accept his lies, they amplified them.

They never viewed his mission as an outright lie, but more of a strategic deception for success. He made statements that arrange the facts to paint the rosiest possible picture. He would spin the truth and mislead his followers because he could, and no one really objected because he was successful.

Your legacy is forever sealed with me if you have followers who are willing to do anything for you, including sacrificing their salvation. You are highly favored and deserve an exceptional place in my kingdom.

I didn't think much of Peter when I first met him. Rev. Ike was far more flamboyant, and Jimmy Swaggart was much more passionate. But Peter had those intangible qualities that can elevate and sustain you longer than the rest.

Peter was weird looking, and sometimes when he preached, he spat the words out the sides of his mouth.

Peter set goals for himself and went after them with a tenacious determination. He had a curiosity for success.

I didn't see Peter as being a long-term asset in my conflict, so I never gave him a large budget. I just sort of allowed him to freelance and make do with what he had.

It turns out that double P was far more cunning than I thought. Within two years, he had turned a bunch of rag-tag cons into a million-dollar business!

He solicited donations to float bibles into the Soviet Union by parachutes, hocked prayer clothes, and pretended to heal the sick.

But his most elaborate scam was that he could speak to God.

I laughed when I first saw it because I could not believe that followers of Christ were that naïve.

He had people believing that God Almighty had given him the ability to see audience members' names, addresses, and illnesses and that he could cure them.

He ran this scam for years, and people were dumping tubs of money at his feet. But like always, all good things must come to an end.

After all, when you're making moves at that rate of speed without the proper guidance, you're bound to make a few mistakes.

It's like playing Jenga. Occasionally, someone will get loose and reckless and cause their tower to wobble and sway. Sometimes it sort-of leans there awkwardly, but most of the time, it crashes to the floor.

Peter's kingdom bypassed the teetering and swaying stage and just collapsed.

A guy named James Randi showed up on the Johnny Carson Show and spilled the beans in intricate detail about his elaborate ruses. They would use aides to gather audience information, and his wife would feed him that information by wireless radio transmission through an earpiece.

You'd think when he got caught, that would have been the end of old double P, but as I stated before, those intangibles can sustain you beyond the lean years.

He declared bankruptcy in 1987, and then went underground.

All I could do was shake my head in disbelief, because lo and behold Thirty-five years later, I see the same guy on late-night TV, selling miracle spring water with the same determined tenacity.

I tossed the remote on the bed and took a sip of Pierre Ferrand Cognac. I walked to the bathroom and added sandalwood and eucalyptus-scented bath oil to the warm water that was already in the jacuzzi tub. The water nearly spilled onto the floor when I climbed in and settled my back against the warm porcelain. The womb-like warmth of the steaming tub overwhelmed my senses and promptly placed me in a relaxed state.

Maybe I got too cocky again. It wouldn't be the first time. After all, modesty has never been part of my DNA.

"So, I guess you're probably wondering who are you and why should I be concerned about you anyway?

Well, I've been called many names over the years. Devil, Satan, Beelzebub, Belial, Father of Lies, Old Serpent, Adversary, Power of Darkness, Tempter, Wicked One Lucifer!

Whatever names your parents or church leaders decided to call me to put fear in your heart, is who I am.

The truth of the matter is you shouldn't be concerned about me because I'm really not a bad person! In fact, I think it's just my reputation that precedes me.

I say that because you see me every day. I'm at your job, in your school, and without a doubt at your church.

I laugh at those pictures of me as some sort of cartoon character in long red underwear with horns and a forked tail, holding a pitchfork. Then there's the one with me as a winged female demon flying through the night, seducing men and attacking pregnant women and infants.

Man, somebody must have had a lot of free time on their hands to come up with those pictures.

The reality is that I don't come dressed like a comical character in red underwear and pointy horns. I come as everything you've ever wished for.

If you want me to be attractive with an engaging personality, I can be that. If you want me to be your best friend with the hottest gossip, I can be that also. I can be whatever you want me to be, as long as you understand that you represent me and not God.

I consider myself a one-stop-shop for all your needs—sort of like a concierge service that specializes in accommodating all your carnal pleasures.

If you crave food, I can feed that limitless appetite until you say when. If you have an itch for a little sexual healing, I got flavors from vanilla to molasses. And if you lack confidence, I have the perfect substances that you can drink, snort, or shoot-up. All made just for putting your confidence level through the roof.

I pride myself on having a no-judgment zone.

My motto is, "I have a lot to offer, and I aim to please."

Not only can I assist you with your carnal desires, but I can also personalize those desires and turn them into necessities and entitlements. I offer excellent customer service, but everything offered comes with a price.

Christians call it temptations so that you have a negative connotation about me. I just give you all the possibilities of what pleasure can be!

There has never been a time in history that I ever forced anything on anyone.

I'm like that little old innocent lady giving away greasy sausages at Sam's Warehouse. I just offer you a sample; one naughty deed per toothpick.

It's not my fault if you overindulge!

I'm amazed at how Jesus gets credit for saving souls, and I get blamed when your life goes up in smoke. It's downright hypocritical if you ask me! All week long, I give you the opportunity to lie, cheat, gossip, and steal, and then you show up to church on Sundays cursing me and singing:

"I beat the devil running and I'm so glad."

Really? Did I force you to sin?

Is that really what you want everyone to believe?

First, you have to be honest with yourself about a couple of things. I just offer what you desire and move on. You can accept what I offer or leave it; it's no skin off my back. But to be perfectly clear, sooner or later everyone accepts my offer. I've only met one person who ignored my barrage of pleasure, and I eventually nailed his ass to a cross.

If I really felt like your little raggedy soul was that important to me, I would press you harder. My resume lists some of the most influential people ever to walk this earth, and every one of them has accepted my offer on at least one occasion: Adam, Eve, Trump, Hitler, Jakes, Osteen, and even your beloved Obama. You probably never seen them fall, but I promise you they fail just like everyone else.

I know every little dirty deed that I convinced them and you to do!

So, I ask you again! Why? Why would I be concerned about you singing God's praises every Sunday?

You think that just because you don't drink, smoke, or commit adultery, that you avoided my traps and snares.

Wrong!

When your classmate posts a picture standing in front of their private beach house, are you proud of their achievements, or are you gripped with that stinging pain of envy?

When Sister Wilson tells you something shameless and unfounded about Mother Brown,

Do you smile and politely say, "That's odd! Mother Brown has always spoken so highly of you."

Or does your curiosity suddenly cause you to listen to a little more chit-chat and call your friends with the latest gossip.

I marvel at how easy the curiosity of good "Christians" causes them to meddle in the lives of others. Nothing is a bigger invitation to sin than a little chitchat about so-and-so?"

"Heads turn, ears perk up, and meddlesome curiosity is immediately incited. Seldom is the news that follows positive. Ninety percent of what you

hear through gossip is none of your business. And yet, curiosity convinces you that you have the right to this information."

My relaxed state began to evaporate as the water started to cool, so I stepped out of the tub. I toweled off and wrapped myself in the over-sized Gucci robe. My mind went back into business mode, as I walked back to my bedroom. Other projects needed my attention: Another war, another virus, and without a doubt more church leaders.

I could still hear Peter Popoff vaguely in the background as I sat on the bed and searched my bag, retrieving my leather diary.

"This faith tool is the miracle spring water, which will help you to see liberation from the bondage of Satan "It's free. I want to send it to you, no obligation. Call me now!"

I was startled by the voice of Popoff growling at an elderly black lady.

"Is that your cane?"

The stunned woman looked at the cane and shook her head, yes. Peter Popoff quickly moved toward the cane and snatched it out of her hands, tossing it towards the pulpit.

"I believe God has given you a divine chiropractic treatment! Amen! Hallelujah! Amen in Jesus's name! You can walk now without the cane. Take a few steps and make Satan mad!"

I gave a quick nod of approval towards the TV and pushed my back into the pillows that were stacked against the wall. I couldn't help but smile in admiration of myself as I casually thumbed through my diary glancing at page after page of impious entry titles of past centuries.

I needed to write something profound, so I thought about what was happening in my life, and all my fears, struggles, and triumphs over the years. And then inspiration struck! I lowered my pencil to a fresh page and began to write.

Dear Diary:

My goal has always been to destroy God's kingdom, and what better way to accomplish that goal than through church leaders.

Why?

Mainly because I got what you call superior in-game intelligence!

Any general serious about success enters a battle with a plan. He knows his adversary's strengths, weaknesses, tactics, and contingencies. If he doesn't, even his best intentions won't keep him from defeat.

I use my superior skills, clever ruses, and temptations to distract you and destroy your relationship with God.

I rarely use outside forces to destroy your relationship with God; Christ-loving folks will do just fine!

I can rip an entire church congregation to shreds in a matter of minutes with a simple rumor.

I can convince the most loyal servants of God to abandon their faith during a moment of rage.

But I inflict the most significant damage on Christ people through their leaders.

I'm always searching for young, easily impressed church leaders who have intelligence, self-confidence, determination, and sociability. Those types of leadership skills I can mold and use to my advantage.

An admired commander such as myself, understands the importance of recruiting the right person for the right leadership position.

Sometimes the difference between a thriving organization and one on the brink of ruin comes down to the leader in place, and people groomed around them.

I always plan with the future in mind. The best way to ensure that my future remains bright is to identify people that have high potential to be successful leaders.

Taking souls from Christ is my business so I run my business like a Fortune 500 company, both in the presentation of myself and my brand.

I need leaders who represent me with big ideas, big initiatives, and big personalities.

Don't get me wrong; I still make offers to church leaders with run-of-the-mill leadership skills. But then again, there's a huge difference between having Lebron James lead your team instead of Darko Milicic.

An average church leader might get an opportunity to preach out of a middle school gymnasium, have a couple thousand Facebook followers, or drop three or four low-budget seminars. Still, I will never elevate you any further.

You have all the skills to be successful, but you're just seeking a platform. I need exceptional leaders seeking a pedestal. Platforms are designed to be shared and used for the benefit of others; pedestals reach beyond that because there's only room for one.

Again, I need a person with phenomenal leadership skills who has a curiosity for success!

Phenomenal leadership skills place you among a very elite group of church leaders like Joel Osteen, TD Jakes, Eddie Long, and yes, Peter Popoff.

All these men started their careers with dreams of just being a good shepherd and spreading God's word.

But it was that curiosity for success that set them apart from everyone else.

Starting a new church is like opening a restaurant: you set out to share your passion for God with others, but there's lots of competition. Your odds of being successful are slim, and most church leaders fail in their first five years unless you're willing to go against the grain. Going against the grain often means forgetting about everything you've been taught and making your own decisions.

All I do is clarify your decision process with the reality of your circumstances. I help you understand that the possibilities of your life can be far better with my guidance.

When I make an offer to someone, consider it the greatest accomplishment of your life. Consider it an honor that you even made it onto my radar. A proposal from me changes the trajectory of your entire life and catapults you into the upper echelon of televangelism. You have the opportunity to earn a six-figure salary in one week, book deals, power, and notability. When you receive an offer from me that means you've made it! You've risen above all the noise and exceeded all expectations, and now you are ready for the big leagues.

I always give my potential leaders, "The Speech".

The speech shows them just how far they've come and what they need to do to maintain the same upward mobility.

My pet-project, Frank, was in a privileged position because he saw firsthand how I elevated his father, Edward, from table scraps to top of the food chain. I expected Frank to fall in line like his father, like Peter Popoff, and like all the rest of the great church leaders that I've placed in positions of power.

Again! A curiosity for success is always the determining factor if I will make him successful.

I gave Frank the same speech that I gave his father, Peter Popoff, and all the other church leaders with great potential and curiosity for success.

I drape my arm across their shoulders like an older fraternity brother and pull them close.

"Young man, you've come a long way!"

"God has blessed you with the ability to woo audiences with your smooth-as-silk voice and powerful oratory skills. Stop missing your blessing because of a couple of melancholy sermons. This is the blessing that you've been praying for! The blessing that you've been tarring for. Why are you wasting all that talent talking about sinning, death, and hell? You sound like an angry prophet! Don't get me wrong, the squeaky wheel gets the oil, but not on this level. On this level, I need refinement, control, stick to the talking points.

"All that palm trees shredding, the rain slanting sideways, the ocean rising like a wall, seven-headed dragon nonsense. You're scaring people away!

Think more Obama and less Trump in your sermons!"

"Being an angry prophet on this level only ruffles the feathers of donors with deep pockets. Now that hope, prosperity, and pie in the sky stuff, that's where you need to be at!"

"Uh, huh, I thought so! It sounds good, doesn't it."

"Hey! But first things first! Before you get a little too excited, let's take a quick look at what I'm going to need from you."

"First off, if you're not willing to stand in front of the masses and tell a couple of white lies, then you need not accept my offer. I'll just banish you to that little storefront ministry, and you can go on your merry way! If you're not willing to lie about small things, how can I trust you to go further and deceive the masses."

"Second! You must have a curiosity for success! Your desire for reverence, wealth, and power must take precedence, even over your desire to save souls. You have to love the altitude! You have to enjoy being on top of the mountain and hunkering down to protect and guard your territory because you represent my brand, and that's what I expect."

"Back in the day, things were a little different between God and me. Spiritual warfare was like playing chess. No six-figure salary or book deals up for grabs: just him sending out his best warriors, and me countering with my best soldiers. God appointed uncompromising church leaders, and they were proactive in developing new leaders. The early church leaders were unselfish and built a wall of Godly choices around their young upstarts that satisfied their spiritual desires."

These new Cash App prophets are much more accommodating to my lures of wealth and power. They care about their selfish desires more than your salvation, and I gladly help them fulfill those needs beyond their wildest dreams. They enjoy the limelight and elevation to a higher pedestal, and they love to look down on others because it makes them feel superior.

Wait a minute! That sounds a lot like me!

I took another sip of cognac and readjusted my pillow and continued thumbing through my diary, searching for another header. My eyes were tired, but I couldn't remember any occasion when I went to sleep in peace and had a full night's rest. My mind was always working, thinking of defensive strategies, calculating losses, and percentages. Remnants of a war that could have been avoided if God would have simply given me more power.

Entry:
The War

I have an unquenchable desire for power. Why, because that's the way I was created. I was never made to sit idly around waiting to follow behind someone, and God should have understood that when our conflict first occurred.

If I can be totally honest, had God satisfied my desire for power, would I have been rebellious?

I've been fighting everyone since the beginning of time, but I never received the accolades like Christ.

God got mad at me for one little thing, and he went straight to the nuclear option.

No punishment! No warning! Just started kicking people out of heaven!

I mean, really! How would you feel about being fired from your job if you were the best at it? That's like kicking Lebron James out of the NBA for being the best.

I was the best, period!

And then what does God go and do? Kick me out and give his little snot-nosed brat authority over everything.

Yeah, it's true! God had a couple of issues with me because I was arrogant and boastful. But can you blame me? He got mad at me for stating the obvious.

I was the most powerful, beautiful, and the wisest angel of all of God's creation. I walked and talked to God every day. I was second only to him, and nobody came close to having as much power and reverence as me. I was the only angel to have ever walked on the fire stones before the Great Throne. When God wanted to get things handled, he called me! When he struggled with hard decisions in the kingdom, he called me.

When I walked by other angels, they bowed to me. I was treated like a king, a savior, and yes, even a God. I was controlling heaven before JC was even an itch in his daddy's trousers, and when little JC was searching for a role model, he was in admiration of me first.

And I can't forget the perks that went along with the title of second-in-command.

Oh my God, the perks were so amazing!

It was beautiful; everything about it screamed luxury; from my automobiles to my four-level penthouse. My duplex home rose majestically above the azure waters on the upper eastside of heaven. Exquisite crystal chandeliers, and a private elevator entrance with security. I had breathtaking views from every room. Wall to wall glass windows and expansive terraces provided me unobstructed views of the Mediterranean Sea and the magical valleys below. At sunset, the valley filled with the most amazing orchestra of jungle sounds, to which I fell asleep. In the morning, the easterly breeze gently cooled me as I sipped a chilled glass of Domaine de la Romanée-Conti.

And when I wanted to hit the streets of heaven, I didn't have to worry about calling the garage to retrieve my car. There was a private elevator for my car, which lowered me to the street level while I was sitting behind the wheel. The only thing that I had to do was peel out without any hassles. I felt like God in my untouchable five-star heavenly castle.

I didn't rebel to destroy anybody, that's just the way it went down. God wanted his Son to be involved in the family business, that was cool with me.

I mean, I understand! Keep it all in the family. He wanted his Son groomed to carry on his legacy.

The problem I had was that he gave him the keys to the kingdom, and he never put in any work. I just didn't think he deserved it. All I said was that God's kingdom wouldn't exist without me, and JC or humans didn't deserve to be over me. I was the one doing all the work, and they never paid any dues to have that title.

Unbeknownst to me, other angels started tattle-telling about what I was saying.

Somebody told Raphael, and he added a bunch of stuff to the story when he told Gabriel and Michael.

It was sort of like that game Chinese whispers. The first person whispers a message to the next person, and that person whispers what he thinks he heard someone else say, and the next thing you know, the message is all screwed up.

Michael added that "He said in his heart, I will ascend into heaven, I will exalt my throne above the stars of God" to get the war going.

He probably felt the same way about JC, but he was just too chicken shit to say anything.

Anytime I see Michael walking around now, I feel like Nino Brown when Kareem screwed up everything.

"Never liked you anyway, Pretty Motherfucka."

The funny thing about the whole situation is that Mike and I were cool when we were younger. We used to hang out and talk about what we would do when we got our wings.

And how did he repay me?

By stabbing me in the back!

Michael had animosity towards me all that time because God saw more potential in me and treated me as such. I tell you, sometimes people will do and say anything to come up when they're low on the totem pole.

By the time Michael got finished telling the story to God, he wanted my head on a gold platter.

I mean, I can't really blame him. Michael made it look like I was out-of-pocket and talking reckless.

But I was definitely not just going to sit around and wait for someone to kill me.

As soon as Michael called me, I knew it was a set-up.

He called me sounding all nice like I had just won the Publishers Clearing House Sweepstakes.

"Hey Lucifer! How's everything going? Great! Hey, God was wondering if you could drop by the throne for a couple of minutes for some fresh baked donuts and conversation. Nobody else will be here except God and me."

Freshly baked donuts my ass!

I knew what Michael wanted! He wanted me to bow down and pledge my loyalty to God in front of the other Angels, right before he hacked my head off.

I started wagging my finger like Mutombo No! No! No! Not today my friend. As soon as I got off the phone, I called up my ride or die angels that had been waiting for the slightest insurrection led by me.

"Let's get it popping baby, it's time to go to war."

We looked like Genghis Khan and the Mongolian Empire when we surrounded the Hill of the Most-High. Angels were running in terror and begging God to do something.

I saw JC peep out the window, but that boy was shaking like a crap game. I could hear him talking loud about what he was going to do to me, but he never came out of the house. Sometimes I wish he came out that house, but God sent Michael.

One on one, I would've beat Michael's ass, but he had a nice little celestial squad of warriors with him. They were fearless and fought as a team, plus I had a couple of soldiers' bitch-up on me and switched sides.

Bottom line, I lost! God's Divine Army led by Michael protected the throne and the big fellow had me stripped of my titles, authority, and kicked out of heaven with my army.

Do you know what Michael whispered in my ear as he was escorting me out of heaven?

"The saddest thing about betrayal is that it never comes from enemies; it comes from those you trust the most. Thanks for keeping the penthouse in such great shape, I hate redecorating."

Fucking prick!

All I could do is smile. He beat me at my own game, and I never saw it coming.

Christians all over the world still rejoice at what happened on that day. Even the Catholic Church made a prayer about Michael during the war.

People often ask me, why didn't I just keep my mouth shut and bow down to God?

I say why?

Picture me sitting in heaven, knowing how great I am but settling just to appease God. I mean, I understand that a more powerful being created me and gave me knowledge!

But how do I know that it was God?

For all I know, God could have appeared on the scene a couple of hours before me and crowned himself God!

So, let me understand this! A person is walking around heaven, claiming that he's God, telling me to bow down to his Son and humans?

"Not I said the fly!"

I tell you like I told Jesus when I spoke to him in the wilderness. There's a reason God made me second-in-command! You might get all the accolades for saving souls, but I can still convince a snail to drink saltwater. And I will always be able to persuade your best and brightest servants to leave you."

I'm not afraid to admit that sometimes I win, and sometimes I lose. But I never hid behind daddy's coattail. I got put out of one kingdom and built mine on earth from scratch. Nobody ever handed me anything. Now that's a man with determination!

I'd rather rule on earth than serve in heaven any day; I'm just not built for servitude!

The only difference between me and JC now, is the kingdoms that we control.

Trust me! I'm not mad about the situation. The big man had to do what he had to do!

But things are a lot different now. As a matter of fact, I'm feeling a lot like Marvin Sapp now.

"I'm stronger, and I'm wiser, I'm better because I made it through my storm and test, all by myself. I don't need anybody else.

Who put this thing together?

Me! That's who!

Who do I trust? Me!

I don't need him; I don't need her; I don't need nobody!

My fault, sometimes I mix the words up with Scarface's speech, but that's what the song sounds like to me when I sing, and that's all that counts.

I'm a supernatural being with remarkable powers in the physical realm. I can make people sick, throw them in prison, and I can even kill them. Nevertheless, my main way of getting my revenge on God is by taking his most loyal servants and repurposing them for my kingdom.

I don't care how spiritually extolled you think you are in the divine world; you cannot compete with me in the physical world.

You have to understand; I was created to be the perfect temptation.

How could a perfectly good being, with perfect goodwill, and a perfectly good heart ever experience an imperfect impulse to be evil? The answer is that God granted me that authority through the same free will as Eve.

Entry:
The Temptation of Eve

The day Eve said yes to me, was the day that the battlefield evened out for me.

You should have seen the way I twisted and turned her reality until she forgot about God's commandments!

Instead of seeking God's permission first, she allowed me to paint an alternate reality based on temptations and stimulations that I controlled.

I started sounding like a walking advertisement for Nike. Anything your heart desires or wants, Just Do It!

Why would you spend time denying and avoiding pleasure, when there are so many temptations that will soothe those desires properly.

Go figure, you're omnipresent, all seeing, all knowing, and you placed two sheep in the world controlled by a wolf.

You had to know what I was going to do. Adam by himself probably could have held his own, but that Eve. As soon as God popped that rib out of Adam, I was plotting and scheming on the best way to destroy everything good in them.

Eve was a sweet girl, but she had to be sacrificed. I could have left her and Adam alone and went about my business, but that's not how I operate. I had an insatiable desire to tinker and twist the gears in her head so that she would go against God's will.

When I first saw Adam and Eve, I was a little intrigued and confused. I found it odd that God had anointed Adam to be the stronger vessel without seeing them interact.

Adam was superior in brute strength, and his adherence to Gods word was stronger.

But I could see that Eve was the driving force behind his development in my realm. Adam was controlled by God's will, and Eve was full of curiosity.

Eve was uninterested in the things that Adam was excited about doing. Adam enjoyed long strolls with God, naming animals, and had no problem doing what God said at face value.

Instead of accepting that Adam would provide for her,

Eve would ask how that would happen!

If God said, don't touch that, she wondered why!

When God instructed Adam to keep Eve away from me, she asked why.

She wanted more out of their relationship, but Adam was incapable of giving her that.

I would speak to Eve occasionally in passing by their garden, and Adam would get protective of her, and run to tell God.

"God, I don't like the way Satan is staring at Eve. It's like he's sizing her up, and then she will look back and smile. It's not right God! Eve is my woman, and I don't want him around her anymore."

God would ask me to please respect the boundaries of Adam and stay away from Eve and the garden, but I never listened.

Whenever I spoke to Eve, I saw that flicker of curiosity in her eyes.

Eve was walking around the Garden of Eden smelling like fresh lavender and glistening with olive oil.

Adam was never taught or shown how to shower Eve's beautiful ass with pure pleasure.

He was so focused on doing the will of God, that he felt comfortable leaving Eve unaccounted for. He understood that they needed to stay fixated on the divine and avoid me altogether. So, Adam built a wall around the garden.

He kept all the beautiful butterflies and cute cuddly poodles in the garden. And turned the ferocious animals lose outside the garden.

He got a kick out of seeing tigers and grizzly bears chase my ass up and down the road. But that still didn't quench Eve's curiosity to know me.

Eve enjoyed watching me play rough and tumble with the panthers and tigers, while Adam was in the shade curled up next to his favorite poodle naming stars.

She was bored with her good little boy, Adam. He tried to keep it interesting, but how many gifts can you give a woman who has everything. Adam was doing the best he could; He clearly loved her, and she loved him.

In his eyes, he satisfied her by giving her anything she wanted, but she was longing for more.

She saw the way I dogged out the female angels near the garden. The way they argued and fought to the death for my attention, and then I'd leave with another one.

She was curious about what I was doing to them. How was I making the fire in them burn so bright for me?

She blushed when I held her gaze and smiled seductively at her.

 I just had to be patient!

I had to give her time to feel that fluttering of butterflies and magnetic pull of romantic attraction.

 God never taught her to guard her thoughts against being hijacked by an attraction so strong that it occupied her mind for hours and days.

He never taught her how to react when she was focused on a task, but a person was still lingering in her thoughts somewhere.

That feeling deep down when you're anticipating the next inter-action. Thinking about the way they talk, wondering about the things they like and dislike.

Nah! God never gave her protection against that, but I was going to give her a hard lesson in it.

By the time I started flirting with Eve, she was fully aware of who I was. She had been warned by God, warned by Adam, warned by the other angels but she just had to know for herself, if that wild, bad-boy, Satan could be tamed.

Eve was at the gate watching me intently as I joked around with some of my fallen angels, and I waved at her. My wave must have caught her by surprise because she immediately started picking up peaches off the ground, placing them in her woven basket, and pre-tending to ignore me.

I told my boys that I would catch up with them later and walked over to the garden gate.

"Whassup Eve, watcha doing?"

She responded as if she were annoyed with me.

"What does it look like I'm doing, I'm busy."

"What's wrong with you?"

She pulled the basket of peaches behind her as if hiding them from me and took a defiant stance.

"Nothing is wrong with me Satan; I just don't understand why you're coming over here and bothering me."

I smiled at her in a flirtatious manner and curled my lower lip inside my mouth before speaking.

"Oh, so you do know my name! Here all this time, I thought you were ignoring me, and you up in that garden checking around for ol' Satan."

Eve jerked her head backward, and her forehead wrinkled as if I had said something insane.

"Boy! Ain't nobody checking around for you. You need to be checking behind all those demon whores you have running around acting stupid for you."

My tongue slowly slid across my lower lip as laughter slowly whizzed from my mouth.

"Yeah! You right, they do be out here tripping, that's why I'm trying to get up in the garden, curl up with you, or play with the poodles like your man."

Eve dropped her basket and briefly bent forward laughing, before bouncing back into her defiant stance with the sweet, angry smile.

I pulled a small rose off one of the vines outside the gate and held it in her direction. Her face softened, and she looked around cautiously, before reaching her hand through the scroll-metal, wrought iron gate.

Thank You!

I handed her the rose, and I held her finger briefly and stared until her eyes collided with mine.

"Wow! You have gorgeous eyes."

I touched several of her fingers and pulled her hand towards me.

I felt her hand tense up as if unsure, but she didn't pull away.

"Eve, I think about you a lot. No matter how many girls you see me running around with, they can't measure up to you. Seriously Eve, I like you! Not just because you're beautiful, but the whole you. You have been here for three weeks, and I really respect the woman that you have become. I'm not trying to cause any problems with you and Adam because that's your man and I know you love him. I'm just trying to have a small part in your life. When Adam is away doing God's work, I just want to be here for conversation. Adam is helping to create a world. I understand what he is doing is important, but you need someone to talk to also, let me be that person."

Her smile hardened and her face became serious as she considered what I was offering. She hesitated for a few seconds and her hand started to tremble slightly as if her curiosity was whispering to take a chance.

Her moment of indecision was interrupted by Adam's shout from a distance, and she quickly pulled her hand away and backed away from the gate.

I moved backward away from the gate, still gazing in her eyes as a bright flirtatious smile crossed my lips.

"You know, you're kind of cute when you don't have an attitude!"

Eve smiled and blushed even harder as I backed further away from the gate.

She walked away, mesmerized with my air of confidence and seductive charm. Her stomach fluttered with keen awareness, and her adrenaline raced as she held the rose close to her nose.

 She had always been warned to stay away from me, and now she realized why. I whistled softly to get Eve's attention, and she turned back towards me.

"Tell Adam to rearrange the alphabet so that U and I are together. I'll see you tomorrow!"

Eve blushed and clenched her mouth tightly to keep from giggling as I walked away.

"Boy shut up! Ain't nobody walking way back over to this gate to see you."

But she did come to see me! She met me at that same locked gate, at the same time, for over a month.

I flirted with her a lot, but most days, we just talked about her situation.

We talked about God, Adam, and her role in the world. Adam wanted to start a family, but she was unsure if she was ready.

Adam had always imagined himself having lots of children because that was something that God wanted him to do. But no one had ever asked how she felt about it. She had only been on the earth a short time, and now Adam was suddenly thrusting this life-altering responsibility on her. She just didn't want to be cooped up in the garden chasing kids around. She was curious about other things in the new world, and she wanted to explore them.

Eve and I could talk for hours about any subject no matter how personal, and then there were days when we could only speak for a short time.

No matter how long or short our time together, she seemed to enjoy her time spent with me genuinely. Given any other circumstance, we probably could have been a good match.

I'm like anybody else! I love being around an attractive woman with great personality. God made Eve with all the intangibles to be the perfect lifelong partner. She had the ability to love and be loved, feel comfortable sharing her innermost feelings, and sharing her dreams.

Once Eve opened up to me, I found her to be carefree with a great sense of humor. And she had no problem cracking a joke about herself, without all the "what about my reputation" issues.

My connection with Eve was growing stronger every day, and her attraction towards me was sprouting fresh seeds of curiosity.

Eve was becoming more trustful of me, but she never invited me into the garden.

I understand that's like God's sacred ground!

"No way, shape or form, are you ever going to get in this garden."

At least that's what Adam said!

But I wondered if Eve felt the same way.

Adam was there for Eve as only he could be. God placed them in each other's lives, and at some point, it just made sense to be together. Eve was intelligent from a spiritual point of view, but she was baffled by the feelings of lustful intimacy. The traits that it took to achieve her spiritual awakening, was a hindrance to understanding that earth-shattering feeling of unrequited love.

The first time looking at someone and feeling an unexplainable urge in the pit of your stomach to risk it all. Heart pounding so loud and fast that you're surprised that someone can't actually see it beating out of your chest. The first time discovering that constant state of delirium that you no longer know what is real. That feeling of not knowing what you are doing, and still doing it. The first time you wanted nothing more in the world than just being with that person.

Unrequited love is silly, crazy, wild, and even foolish. You don't plan it, you don't control it, you don't force it. You just close your eyes and take the plunge.

Eve didn't understand where those feelings were coming from, but again I was willing to give her a hard lesson about them.

I understood if I took away that type of connection, she would start to question herself.

"Is Adam really the right man for me, or is it Satan?

This question has been asked for thousands of years, and it's always the same answer.

The grass is never greener on the other side of the fence; it just seems that way when your grass doesn't appear very green.

While Adam's grass may have been a dull green, at least it was real. Adam was created to be the man of Eve's dreams, but that was without temptation and lust.

My perfect smile, my perfect scent, the right words said at the right moment. Everything about me was counterfeit but she could only see the qualities that Adam did not have.

The reality was that I could have never given her half of what Adam had given her.

The only thing that I could offer Eve in a relationship was covetous desire.

Eve already had a connection with Adam, and she allowed me to break that bond. Instead of keeping her mind focused on God, supporting Adam, and trusting God's process, she became curious about me.

Eve had never experienced that feeling of agonizing over someone until you can barely breathe. That paralyzing loss of a special person in your life.

I needed Eve to feel the human pain of rejection to accomplish my goal of entering the garden.

I stayed away from the garden for several days. Eve was human and not divine like me, so her mind was an emotional wreck. Spending all that time together, and then suddenly ghosting her, gave her a feeling of emptiness.

As the saying goes, "you never know what you could have had until it's gone."

She was curious about why I had not come around the gate in days. Who was I with, and what was I doing with them? That jealousy, anger, and lust began to build slowly as she speculated about me.

It was like I was out of sight, but still trapped in her mind!

When I finally decided to see her, I walked toward the gate whistling like the world was mine, and it infuriated her.

She tried her best to ignore me, but I would not allow her to dodge that emotional connection to me.

I spoke to Eve as if nothing was wrong, and as if I had just noticed her.

"Oh! Hey Eve, what's up! I didn't even see you over there! How are you feeling today, beautiful!"

Eve's mood consisted of a combination of excitement and anger. She was excited because she had missed me so much. It seemed like forever since she had last seen me, rather than mere days. Her heart pounded with eagerness because I had become a special presence in her life. She enjoyed spending all her free time with me, and all that had just suddenly vanished.

On the other hand, she was angry with me because I stopped coming around. She knew I was fucking around with different angels, but why did I take that time away from her to do so? She thought our time together was exclusive!

My absence left an empty feeling that resonated deeply within. She had come to the garden's gate every day searching for me, and every day she returned home unhappy. Adam sensed something was troubling Eve, but she refused to talk about it. Day after day of nothing but a slow and steady burn of misery and gloom, and there was absolutely nothing she could do to stop it. It was like trying to hold water with her bare hands, and it slowly dripping away, eventually leaving her with nothing. She couldn't understand why I had to be so selfish when she was trying to understand her feelings towards me.

Why did I have to be such a selfish, uncaring, asshole!

She walked up to the gate to greet me, but I continued walking until I passed by the gate.

At first, she looked as if she was shocked. Her facial expression was saying, "How dare you pass by me, do you know who I am?"

I continued walking a few more steps and turned to her.

"Sorry Eve, I can't talk right now because I have to take care of something. I'll catch up with you some other time."

Eve's response made it clear that her mindset was right where I needed it to be. The hurt, rejection, or frustration had transformed any feelings that she had toward me into anger.

"Oh! Ok, so that's how we're doing things now! I thought we were in a good space! I was giving you a chance to prove that you had some type of decency in you, but I should have known. You're the same old self-indulgent person you've always been. I don't know why I even gave you a chance to be in my life."

I looked back at her and could see the anger boiling inside her. She was screaming insult after insult in my direction, and the Cheshire grin on my face only intensified her rage.

She looked like a beautiful, caged, lioness, aching to be released from captivity as she pointed angrily at me through the wrought iron gate.

"You ain't shit! And everything about you is counterfeit! You walk around screwing everything that moves, and you expect people to respect you. I see why God kicked you out of the garden because everything you touch you either hurt or destroy. I would never want a person like you in my life!"

I felt like Randy "macho man" Savage during an interview, "Ohhhhh, yeahhhh, that's what I'm talking about!"

I needed Eve to lose control of her emotions and get angry because that could potentially affect her thought process.

The first thing that Eve should have done when she started getting angry was stay silent and keep her composure. She should have forced herself to think rationally, and then she would have probably realized what my intentions were. Simply by taking a few seconds to weigh the pros and cons of arguing with me would have surely given her the correct insight.

But instead, she allowed her anger to consume her. The lust and anger blinded her ability to reason, and that was an opening for me.

My eyes narrowed, and I quickly moved toward her and banged my hand against the gate so hard that Eve tripped and fell when she jumped backward.

"Your life!"

"Since when has it ever been your life?"

My voice trembled with emotion, and tears slowly began to fill my eyes as I continued.

"You stay protected behind this gate, while my heart aches just to have a tiny portion of your love. Kicked me out of the garden! And what reason did Mr. Perfect Adam give you for me being kicked out of the garden? Do you think it had something to do with me disobeying God? Noooo! You have it all wrong. God didn't kick me out of the garden because of disobedience! He kicked me out because of my love for you. Now there! I said it! I love you Eve, but I can never have you. But you're right! It's your life! I guess you say, to hell with my feelings! As long as you can hide behind that damn gate, and see me when it's convenient for you, I should be happy. Well, I'm not! I mean, how did you really think this was going to end? Did you just think that you could just touch my hand a couple of times through the gate, and I would be fine?"

I slowly backed away from the gate gasping for breath and cursing as if angry, because she had forced me to pour my feelings out to her.

"I'm sorry! That's just not how my feelings are made!"

Eve discreetly wiped a tear from her eye and folded her arms across her stomach, as I turned to walk away.

I was willing to keep walking. Hell, I had nothing to lose. I had been babysitting her for the past thirty days. Without Netflix! I will be damned if I was going to do another thirty days without any results. I would've just figured out another way.

It was at that moment that I heard the most beautiful sound that I had ever heard.

No, not a bird, or the far-away sound of an angelic choir singing, but the sound of a locked gate latch popping open.

I stopped and immediately turned around, not believing if I heard correctly.

The cringe of the rusty gate opening echoed loudly across the garden.

Eve's eyes were filled with tears, and there was a look of compassion mixed with regret written across her face, as she walked away, allowing the gate to swing open.

In a way, I felt sorry for Eve because she had no idea what I was capable of doing.

The only thing that Eve had to do was say no. I have no intention of fighting a person who is fully prepared for war. I only specialize in sneak attacks.

On the other hand, if you invite me in because you're confused about your feelings, rest assured I will make myself right at home. And Eve's mind was a ball of confusion!

I slowly walked through the gated entrance admiring not only the beauty of the garden but the beauty of Eve.

I could see why Adam wanted God to keep me away from her.

She was gorgeous!

Her long curvy legs complimented the sexy, sway of her ample ass. Tall, thin, with creamy caramel skin, and curly black hair, I couldn't help but be attracted to her. Or should I say lustful of her?

I pulled the gate shut behind me and followed quietly behind her. It almost felt like I was being toyed with as she took me further into the garden, finally stopping in a secluded area.

I could feel the butterflies fluttering in my stomach as I got closer to her. It could've been gas, but Old Satan felt pretty special that day because I was about to do what only I could do best. Corrupt one of God's creations!

Eve looked at me with an anxious smile.

I extended my hands and without saying a word, she took them. I pulled Eve into my arms and hugged her. The smell of fresh lavender and raspberries crashed my senses as I took a deep breath and exhaled deeply with approval.

"You smell amazing!"

She responded with a petite voice, that was barely above a whisper.

"Thank you!"

I could feel her tense body suddenly relax, as I wrapped my arms even tighter around her. She had never felt this protected before. She probably thought that I was incapable of making her feel this way. Before today, her opinion was that I flirted with different women, got what I wanted, and kept going. Adam thought that building a wall around Eve was what made her feel protected, but it wasn't. Protection was holding her body close to mine, pulling her head to my chest, and swaying gently as if listening to Déjà vu by Teena Marie.

Eve told me that Adam and God were on a quest near Egypt, and I lied and told her that I had just been in the same area looking to build a new home. It didn't matter what we were talking about; all she could feel was the warmth of this thing called affection.

I tried to separate just to look into her eyes, but it was like she was afraid to let go. She gazed up at me shyly and whispered, "This feels nice".

I couldn't help but notice the huge smile splattered across her face. She looked like the teenager who just found out that the captain of the basketball team was asking her for a date. She had to admit that it was exciting that another man found her attractive. Eve had never felt like Adam was attracted to her. She was so used to him fumbling and flailing his way to a quickie, that she had no idea that there was this beautiful thing called passion attached to it. Something as minor as just gazing at her affectionally made her feel attractive.

She loved how I made her feel. Her body had been starving for this type of attention, and finally, she was receiving it.

I grabbed her hands gently but firmly and placed them in front of her and paused. I could tell that she was nervous because she was trembling.

"Do you mind if I kiss you?"

Her breathing slowed as she blushed and gazed slowly at the ground. She swallowed hard and shook her head in the positive.

I cupped her face in my hands, came close, and looked in her eyes. She was beautiful, and her eyes carried an expression of an innocent and uncertain girl. It was like she was exploring her sexuality for the first time.

I held her tight and I could feel her heart was pounding against her chest. Her skin quickly warmed and turned moist as I lowered my head and Eve parted her lips. I closed my eyes and took a deep breath and slowly breathed out.

I kissed her like she wanted to be kissed, like no being had ever kissed her before. Soft, moist, and hot! Unlike Adam, I wasn't trying to win a battle. I was seeking closeness and sharing one timeless and passionate moment. The heat rose in her cheeks as her tongue touched mine, quick, electric, and delicious. The kiss blew her thoughts to smithereens, shutting down her brain until she was nothing but silly putty in my arms. Eve didn't care if I was Satan anymore! She didn't care that she would fall for me and that I would eventually break her heart. She just wanted to hold onto what she was feeling at that moment.

After a minute of kissing Eve, it was apparent that she wanted to go further. Her arms were wrapped around my upper back, and her body had gone beyond the point where it could let her brain make decisions for it. She had never been seduced before. She wanted me on top of her, inside her, ravaging her like an animal. Why shouldn't she go for it! No guilt, no commitments, no analyzing what was happening.

She had always gone for the safe option, and I was the complete opposite of safe. Wildly attractive, devilishly sexy, clearly a confidant womanizer. Why not let go and enjoy herself for once in her life.

I pinned her against a tree and hovered over her with one hand on the tree and the other hand on her waist. Her breath caught as her arms curled around my shoulders. Her body felt like a raging furnace as I pushed my hard penis between her thighs and teased her.

She quivered and twitched with each movement until she grabbed the back of my neck and buried her face in my chest. Her cheeks were flush, and her eyes were tightly shut. I wrapped my arms around her body and allowed her to enjoy the moment. Her body was begging her to let me have my way with her. She dug her fingernails into my back and moaned with ecstasy as she swiveled against my hard penis. Her body shivered as I forced her breasts up and together and began sucking. She moaned as I slurped and gently teased each nipple until they were swollen like luscious berries.

I gently cupped her rear and lifted her until she was on her tiptoes. I ran my hand down the curves of her thighs, urging her to wrap her legs around my waist. My throbbing manhood was ready to pierce deep inside Eve's soft, silky, opening.

Her body suddenly tensed up with fear, and she tried to push herself away. I tightened my grip, holding her more securely against me.

"I can't!" She gasped, as she shook her head no.

I could tell that Eve was struggling with what she should do. It surprised her how easily she could lose control of her body. Her body wanted her to go further, but she was afraid that she wouldn't be able to stop.

She pawed at my chest, pleading.

"You need to go! Please, Satan let me go."

Tears filled her eyes.

" Please Satan, I can't do this!"

Frustrated as to why she wanted me to stop, I looked deep in her eyes and whispered, almost pleading.

"Baby, what is it? Tell me what's wrong? We both want this, let's just give each other what our bodies are aching for."

Clearly in a panic, she began to squirm fiercely in an attempt to push away.

No!

 I can't!

Satan please, just go before Adam comes back! I don't know what he would do to you.

Angry that Eve had the audacity to insinuate that Adam would somehow hurt me, triggered a response that I still regret to this day.

"Adam?!"

"Who, and what the fuck is an Adam going to do to me!"

"Let me explain something to you! I'm not here to fuck your life up, because it's already fucked up! That motherfucker got your stupid ass locked behind a wall, while he walks around doing what the fuck he wants with whoever. I didn't even ask to be involved in this situation; you were the one who opened the gate. But after the way I had your body twitching and jerking, it's obvious that your precious "Adam" ain't satisfying you. I know you want me! You're just trying to convince yourself that you don't. Stop being immature and let a real man satisfy you."

There was a long awkward moment of silence, and her face grew stoic.

I know, I fucked up!

Maybe I shouldn't have said what I said, but hell, that's what I was feeling. And the reality is I have zero filters, so sometimes I can come off as an asshole.

Eve was struggling with her feelings because of her relationship with God and Adam, and now she realized that I was not the person that I portrayed myself to be from afar.

She decided in that short interaction with me that she had made a huge mistake. She was right in pushing me away because she was sensible enough to know the difference between what's easy and what's right!

In my mind, she was emotionally unavailable. She wanted to "have her cake and eat it too", by toying and taunting the great Satan.

In my mind, she was saying, "You're not going to get what I can give you. I'll make you think I'm available, but in the end, you'll get nothing. I'll leave you craving for me."

Can you imagine that? Satan being left with blue balls!

I stared at Eve, waiting for a response, and she appeared to be aggravated with my comments. It was like I had pulled off a mask and become an annoying, scheming, sleazy person.

I had done everything I needed to do with Eve to seduce her. Given her a big smile, complimented her, and punched all the buttons that elicit strong emotional contact. And after all of that, she was pushing me to the sleazy-person zone.

Was I really that obnoxious?

I tried to apologize, but the more I talked, the more I realized that Eve had somehow lost her attraction towards me and that she was more concerned about how to de-escalate the situation. I mean really?! Eve was staring at me cautiously like I was some crazed stalker that had her cornered. I could see the gears slowly moving in her mind, finally figuring me out.

"Why did I even let this guy in the garden! Ok, just keep calm! I don't want this maniac to go crazy! Why didn't I just listen to God and Adam about this creep! Ok! Just keep calm."

She even had the nerve to start talking to me like a person with a mental health condition on the verge of a mental breakdown.

"Satan, you're an awesome person, but I feel we would make better friends. I do enjoy your company because you always make me laugh. But I can't get involved with you romantically. I'm a married woman and I don't want to complicate things with Adam. I hope you don't take this personal, but right now, I'm terrified of you! You were always so lighthearted and cheerful when you came around. I'm sorry that you took things the wrong way, but I just don't want you to go crazy and start stalking or trying to hurt me."

She placed her hand on my shoulder and continued talking to me like a concerned television host dealing with a family member with serious emotional problems.

"I hope you understand! At the time, I was just lonely, and Adam was gone all the time. I just needed someone to talk to, and you were there. I hope we can still be friends because I don't want to lose your friendship.

My demeanor was calm, but inside was a whole different story.

I was smiling and shaking my head in agreement, but in my mind, I was saying. "I should punch this bitch in the throat."

 I spent all this time coming over to this gate babysitting this pussy, and this is my prize? Being accused of being a stalker!"

I can't say her rejection hurt me, but I was definitely embarrassed. What was the world coming to if I couldn't seduce a weak human?

I had the perfect plan! Get in the garden, seduce Eve, and break her bond with Adam. Adam would have blamed God and in turn, broken his bond with him.

That green-eyed, jealous, demon would have crawled inside Adam and scraped its claws along the pit of his stomach, consuming every inch of his body until it burned away all logic and good feelings.

All that would've remained is hatred, irrational anger, and resentment towards Eve and God.

Eve grabbed my arm and started pulling me as if she were ready to escort me out of the garden. I remained composed and followed behind her, but my mind was scanning in search of a plan B.

We came to the main path of the garden, and I saw a small koi pond with a large tree behind it.

That was it! That was the forbidden tree that my spies had been telling me about.

"And the LORD God commanded the man, saying, 'Of every tree of the garden you may freely eat; but of the tree of the knowledge of good and evil you shall not eat, for in the day that you eat of it you shall surely die."

I immediately detoured away from Eve and made a beeline toward the tree.

Eve turned around and screamed my name in a confused, nervous manner.

"Satan, What? Where are you going?"

My evil side wanted to tell her the truth!

"Like, what do you think I'm about to do? I'm about to destroy your life!"

But I still had to be convincing. After all, what good would it do only to have one-half of God's creations fall? I wanted revenge! I wanted God to experience the hurt and embarrassment that I felt when I was so rudely banished from my plush accommodations in heaven to the misery of Earth.

Yeah! I needed revenge in the worse way.

My mind continued to curse at God as I walked closer to the Tree of Knowledge of Good and Evil.

My focus was broken by Eve screaming in my direction as if panicking and regretting she had allowed me in the garden.

"Satan, where are you going? You can't just be walking around the garden and doing what you want. God has certain rules, and that tree is off-limits. Please don't go over there. Come back over here!"

I rolled my eyes toward the sky in frustration and turned towards Eve. She was running in my direction and waving her hands frantically as if shooing a child from a priceless vase at an art exhibit.

I smiled as if someone had carved a wide grin on my face like the joker, and then I held my hands up as if I were arrested.

"My bad! I'm not trying to cause any problems with you and God; I just got carried away. I was just admiring the beauty of the garden."

Eve was running so fast that she stumbled while trying to stop and avoid me at the same time. I held my arms out and softly cradled Eve as she struggled to regain her balance. She pushed me back uncomfortably, embarrassed that she had almost fallen.

She took two clumsy steps backward and managed a nervous smile. I returned her smile with one of my own and moved forward, pulling her towards me at the same time.

She nudged my chest awkwardly as if to push me backward, but I continued to hold and stare into her eyes. She began to breathe heavily as she wrestled with more urgency, to break my grip.

I tilted my head sideways and smiled as I continued toying with her by grinding against her playfully. Embarrassed by the way I was making her feel, she quickly pulled away and started walking, annoyed at my behavior.

She finally understood that I was not in the garden just to disclose my feelings to her. I was there for ulterior motives. In her heart, she wanted me to leave, but it was much too late for that now. Like most sinful deeds, you swear that you'll never let me in, and then later find yourself regretting that you allowed my suggestions to invade your thoughts, after sinning.

Eve had several opportunities to scream, "keep walking Satan, I don't want anything to do with you." But it was much too late for that now. She had opened the gate and allowed the king of lies, monarch of deceit, emperor of duplicity, to run free in her most secret place, and there was no turning back.

"Eve."

Eve turned around confused, angry, and nearly in tears because she did not know how to get rid of me. She probably could have called to God and he would have saved her, but she was terrified with guilt and fear.

What would God do? What would Adam think of her? How many times had God told her to flee from me? How many times had God told her to keep the gate locked no matter what?

God warned them about having conversations with me. God knew what my capabilities were because he had given them to me. God probably should have stressed that more to Eve, that I was not just a metaphor, but that I was a real person armed with mystical powers.

Now here I was, live and in-person with an arsenal of ruses, twisting and turning Eve's mind, searching for the right combination.

I quickly switched from a seducer full of passion to a kowtowing ingrate.

"Eve, I'm just playing with you! I'm trying to see where your head is at. I mean, I would be lying if I didn't state the obvious about you being beautiful. But that's not why I'm here. God wanted me to test you to see if you would remain faithful to Adam. And I have to be honest with you, I was worried for a moment, but I should have known that you would pull through and turn me down."

Eve looked at my face as if searching for my real intentions but uncertain if she believed me.

"Not only are you beautiful, but you have that special, innate ability to see beyond all the smoke and mirrors and see the traps that I tried to set for you. When I tell God how special you are and how much knowledge you already have, he will probably reward you beyond your wildest dreams."

I fell to both knees and bowed low to the ground, pressing my face against the dark, rich dirt.

"I now understand why God created humans, especially the woman. God created you for a special purpose, and now I clearly see what that is. You truly are the magnificence of God personified in a human form. What an asset, what a helpful person, what a co-worker, what a companion, what an intellectual giant. You have descended out of heaven from God, having the glory of God; and your light is like unto a stone most precious, even like a jasper stone, clear as crystal. Such light emanates from you and it is the most precious, most beautiful, and exquisite. You are the queen of all creation, power above all not blinding or scorching."

And blab, bla, bla, bla! I continued running off at the mouth with one obsequious compliment after the next until her anger and distrust turned into a trance of trust.

We've all heard the old saying, "flattery will get you nowhere." Sometimes I wonder; did the first person who made that statement do it in banter, because flattery definitely works, and it works remarkably well. And more than that, flattery is almost always connected to a bigger lie.

From my perspective, flattery has to be one of the most overused techniques in my arsenal of tricks.

People love to be praised, held in high esteem, and have their egos stroked. Face it, we've all succumbed to this temptation at one time or another, but in the hands of a manipulator such as myself who understands how to use this character flaw, it's simply overpowering.

I am a habitual practitioner of the art of telling people what they most want to hear, and the lower the self-esteem, the more valuable and effective it is.

I tell an uncouth idiot like Donald Trump that he is complex and smart. I tell the Shanaynay faced girl that I enjoy basking in her beauty, and they eat it up.

I flooded Eve with so much flattery that she was embarrassed for me.

"Wow Satan! I never thought that you and God had that type of respect for me. I always just saw myself as Adam's helpmate, and now I find out that I am actually more to Adam than I had ever imagined."

I gawked at Eve and nodded my head up and down like a super fan, thinking to myself.

"Yeah, that's right! Eat that shit up. And if you liked that, you'll love what I'm about to do."

I looked around the vast garden and pointed as if I were peering into outer space.

"Eve, I walk past this garden every day and you're alone, while Adam is off someplace new with God naming the stars.   You stay cooped up in this garden and he comes and goes as he pleases. You eat from the same fruit trees day after day, week after week. I'm allowed to eat from any tree in the world, including in your garden."

I walked over to the Tree of the Knowledge of Good and Evil and gave a swift yank to one of the fruits hanging low.

"And you know why that is?

"Knowledge!"

I started pacing back and forth as if I was teaching a college philosophy class, occasionally stopping to bite the fruit.

"What you learn about the world around you is everything. Even God would agree. Why do you think the Fruit of Knowledge is forbidden? Because of its power! Look at what God has made of the world in just seven days. If you really want to accomplish anything in life and be powerful, you need knowledge. Power is a means to an end, and those who have power understand how to control their world through knowledge."

I walked over to the tree and caressed the dark bark as if I was patting a cute puppy.

You can't control anything in your world if you don't have knowledge. This tree can give you and Adam an understanding of how your world works. It will also give you the same insight that God has and possibly even deeper. You will finally have the edge you need to survive without God."

I yanked another fruit off the tree and Eve cringed and then shook her head in disagreement, but she was still enamored at how rebellious I dared to be. She moved backward slowly and looked in the air as if a lightning bolt was about to strike me.

"Oh my God Satan! What are you doing? This can't be right! God said that we could eat from all the other trees in the garden, but not that one. He said we would die if we ate fruit from that tree."

She turned away and started walking, shaking her head as if she felt sorry for me.

I softly called her name as if I were telling her a secret.

"Eve! Eve! Come here, it's important!"

What Eve should have done was keep walking. She should have started running as fast as she could away from me, but she didn't. She turned around for a split second and glanced in my direction. Her eyes were beaming with curiosity, and she tried to hide the joy and embarrassment written across her face as she walked back to me.

Baam! That quick! I had her set up for a downfall. God told Adam and Eve not to touch the tree no matter what. It's so strange, because I've seen that same sparkle of curiosity for thousands of years, and I still get excited about it because now it's game time. You know it's wrong, but you talk yourself into believing it's right. This is the time when God and I are battling head to head for a soul. This is the time that I dig deep into my bag of tricks and come up with something that will convince you to disobey God.

The thought of deceiving Eve had my palms sweating because this could potentially change God's plan.

"Eve, let me show you something!"

She was nervous and looked around frantically as I pulled her closer to the Tree of the Knowledge of Good and Evil. The full-flavored, hearty, aroma dug deep into her senses as I leaned in and whispered in her ear.

"You walk by the tree of good and evil every day, knowing you want a bite. There is absolutely nothing in this garden that can compare to this creamy, mouth-watering explosion. Here, taste it!"

I took another bite and slowly guided her mouth towards the fruit until she took a bite. The rich, creamy brittle, crème brûlée-like surface was a saccharine cloud of indiscernible flavor. The sweetness and texture approached something close to whipped honey, and it practically dissolved in her mouth. No ice cream or whipped cream was needed!

She paused and closed her eyes as if in a trance.

Mummm! This is so good!

I held the fruit close to her lips, and she took another slow deliberate bite, and then stopped mid-chew.

Oh my God! We shouldn't be doing this!

I pulled her close and gently messaged the side of her neck.

"Why? There's nothing wrong with what you're doing. All you're doing is eating from the best tree in the garden, gaining knowledge, and becoming more powerful. Do you not know that God has eaten from this tree? Hell, I would eat from this tree every day if I lived in this garden."

She shook her head no and looked around apprehensively, almost unsure of what to do next. I could see the guilt and regret beginning to settle in slowly. I had to act quickly, and I whispered to her.

"Look at me, look at me Eve! Does it look like I'm dying? Do you really think God will kill you? He made you in his image, and made me bow down to you? He's not going to hurt you, and he loves you. I tell you what, if you don't believe me, take a piece of this to Adam. I bet he won't care. Besides, if you get Adam to eat a piece, God can't destroy both of you. Come on girl, you know how much God loves you and Adam."

Eve's curiosity of the Tree of Knowledge of Good and Evil made it easy for me to use her sense of reason. I appealed to her ego and placed her on the level of God.

I was an inexperienced snotty-nosed brat back then, but you could tell I had potential as I continued my first temptation speech.

"Listen Eve! The problem is that you don't love yourself! When we don't love ourselves, we are blocked from feeling the love of others. What does that mean? We can't receive God's love. How do I know this? I experienced it. God put me out of paradise not because I was disobedient. He put me out of heaven because I had too much initiative. I wanted my kingdom, and he saw that I had enough resourcefulness to achieve that goal. Think about it! God put the Tree of Good and Evil in the same garden that you live in. He eats from it, I ate from it, why not you? I'll tell you why you can't eat from it! You don't have enough self-love to stand up to God. God made you, so proclaim that you are worthy to hold space. He gave you dominion over everything, act like you own everything. Instead of sneaking around, and asking him what you're allowed to do, take it! If you want a piece of fruit, take it! If you want to achieve greatness, go achieve greatness because you now have that knowledge."

I could see the knowledge of herself slowly creeping forward. She began to look around as if asking, what is happening? She was asking herself questions. She was listening to her thoughts, she was seeing herself walking and occupying space. She was thinking, and the thoughts were in thousands of vivid colors.

When Eve finally saw the person she was, she was embarrassed. She felt like a mindless child, created by God as amusement for Adam. I could kind of understand all the angry thoughts swirling around in her head as she pulled more fruit from the tree.

She asked me to leave and I agreed!

But as an instigator of chaos, I would have been less then truthful had I left without giving my final opinion about the situation. Inside every woman is a crazy, immature girl just waiting to be released, and I thought that this was the perfect time for her to be released.

"Eve! Have you ever noticed how God only communicates with Adam? Why is that! I mean, does he even respect you? You are not just a sexual object or some ignorant child. You are worth more than that! You were created to be a partner to Adam and not a slave. You were created to provide strength and support to him, not to be used and manipulated by them. There's nothing wrong with submitting to them, but don't become a fool in that process. You have your dignity and self-worth. Never sacrifice that!"

I exited the garden, just as God and Adam were returning from their quest. I gave them a friendly smile and waved. Adam and God stared in my direction suspiciously as I walked further down the road. God whispered to Adam.

"Make sure you keep this gate secure. Something doesn't feel right!"

He walked in the opposite direction, and Adam opened the gate to the garden with the key around his neck. Adam closed the gate behind him and gave it a secure yank to make sure the gate was locked.

Adam called for Eve, but she did not answer, and when he finally saw her, he was surprised. Before he left, she was goofy, kind of clumsy, and she never really paid attention to her looks. Now she seemed to take note of her characteristics. She was more aware of the way she looked, walked, talked, and acted.

She was very focused and very convincing as she told Adam about her experience with the forbidden fruit. Of course, Adam was indecisive when first presented with my lure. But you have to understand, curiosity can lead to the biggest sins.

Eve whispered in Adam's ear.

"This fruit has given me insight like I've never had before. Just look at me. Look at me!"

Adam had to admit; there was a certain glow about her. He was curious about the change that he saw in his wife. Her answers were more responsive, and her talk was intelligent.

Could the fruit from that tree really improve on who he already was?

Adam's curiosity was satisfied when Eve whispered in his ear.

"It will make you equal to God! We won't have to depend on him for anything anymore. We can do what we want, go where we want and answer to no one."

Adam was trembling with indecision as he took a bite of the fruit. In his mind, Eve was looking out for him. She was doing what was in their best interest. But, in reality, she was being used by me to make Adam fall. I'm not sure what God expected him to do; after all, she was his partner. And her eye-opening experience with the fruit had altered her into a more powerful, cunning being.

They continued eating the fruit from the Tree of Knowledge and staring into each other's enlarged pupils as they gained more knowledge of themselves.

When God came to the garden, I could only imagine the concern on his face when he saw the two people that he loved and cared for most looking and acting differently.

They were aware of their appearance, gazing at each other for the first time and realizing who they were. They were aware of their actions and they realized that their curiosity was responsible for their separation from God. There are many interpretations of how God punished Adam and Eve. Toiling to grow food, labor pains, the poor snake having to crawl on his belly. But the most significant consequence was their separation from God.

They talked to God daily. God gave them knowledge firsthand, commanded them to take care of the earth, fill and cultivate the planet by following the blueprint God had given them in the garden. They were as nearly perfect as can be imagined because they were made in the image of God.

But their ultimate downfall was their curiosity.

Do you remember that curiosity for success, money, and power that made and destroyed Peter Popoff? It was the same curiosity that made Adam and Eve turn away from God.

Let's examine how that same curiosity was used on my pet-project and his family!

Entry:
The Barkley's

Curiosity originates in fear and in a desire to control the world around you, by knowing where the threats or opportunities are. One could argue that my pet project, Frank and his father Edward, also had a healthy amount of curiosity. Curiosity is the one thing that helps you gain vast amounts of knowledge. But it can also lure you into dangerous places and down risky paths by tempting you to stick your nose into places that your nose has no business being. There are countless examples in history and stories of how too much curiosity can be destructive. Eve would be the first, but she certainly would not be the last.

Frank would have probably followed in the footsteps of his father with a life of luxury and nobility had he only followed my plan, and that plan was simple!

Curiosity leads to temptation! Temptation leads to sin! Sin leads to more sin! Sin leads to a game of "congregation follow the church leader!"

Now just how God used an innocent little girl to destroy months and years of preparation and planning is beyond me!

I had that boy Frank right where I wanted him, and I be damned if he got away.

Frank was the Director of Youth Ministry at St. Stephens Pentecostal Church, in Cincinnati Ohio. He was assigned to this position because of his love for Christ and the calling that God had on his life. Every Sunday, he was charged with bringing the word of God to the young saints in the flock. And every Sunday, he did a superb job of making sure they received God's word.

Like his father, Edward, I had satisfied his curiosity and convinced him to walk away from Christ. I had broken him down so skillfully that he would've been under my control as a church leader, which means that a newly ordained and respected church leader would be working for my team and ministering to God's flock. Matthew described them as ravenous wolves in sheep's clothing.

I probably would not have expected Frank to be a "ravenous wolf," but I would have definitely encouraged him to give out a few tainted shots of the gospel. I can just imagine Frank standing in front of twenty thousand people, "convincing them that even hell doesn't seem half bad if you don't have to go there now."

To understand how I twisted Frank's curiosity into sin, you have to understand my history with Frank's father.

Like any great church leader that I've encountered, Edward Barkley started with good intentions. He was the perfect representation of Christ. Everything that he did was matched perfectly in line with the word of God. He had reverence for God and wanted nothing more than to please him through all that he did. He spent most of his free time reading the bible and praying, but his number one passion was winning souls for Christ.

Like Frank, I did not attack Edward when he was strong in Christ, I attacked when he was at his weakest and made him start questioning his faith.

Cincinnati OH in the nineties and early 2000s was a hotbed for servants of Christ.

Edward never had formal training in theology, but he could connect with the congregation emotionally. Edward was saved, sanctified, and filled with the holy ghost in his early twenties and eventually, he was ordained to be a minister.

The small Pentecostal church where he got saved took the words written in the bible literally. That meant that once you accepted Jesus Christ as your personal savior, your life was forever changed. Having your name written in the Lamb's Book of Life, meant that you were part of an exclusive family. The outside world no longer existed, and your only concern was being ready when Christ came back.

Like his son, Edward believed that if he could just talk to you about Christ, your life would be forever changed. And in some ways, that was true. Edward's non-confrontational style of delivering the word of God was what people were seeking. And he was also fearless about where he was willing to take the word. You must understand, spiritual warfare is difficult and dangerous, and sometimes you have to play on the opponent's field.

Late night on Linn St., in front of the Parktown Café, was usually where you could find Edward witnessing about Jesus Christ in the middle of the carnival atmosphere unleashed on the streets every Friday and Saturday night.

This man was amazing! Some people were annoyed when he first started, but he eventually became a peaceful fixture in a sea of unadulterated debauchery. The drug dealers protected him and demanded that outsiders give him respect. You were sadly mistaken if you thought you would get away with treating Edward like trash.

There had been many nights that my wolves came out of the club drunk and belligerent towards Edward.

"Shut up! Nobody wants to hear all that Jesus bullshit this time I night. Man, take that shit across the street, before I put one of these hot ones in ya' ass."

It would only take a few minutes to get back to the shot callers roaming the block, and those poor loudmouths would be surrounded by goons questioning what their problem was. Edward would just calmly separate the parties and flash that big annoying smile.

"Come on, brothers! Blessed are the peacemakers for they shall be called the children of God."

And the crowd would disperse.

Edward reminded me of Daniel in the lion's den. Daniel was a good man, but he was not the hero you think he was. When Darius the Mede sentenced Daniel to one night in club lion's den, that boy was shaking like a crap game. He was so terrified when he heard those hungry lions, I could have sworn that his knees buckled.

But I must give it to Daniel; he played it cool. Even if he was scared, he didn't look it. That boy was in the lion's pit doing the "Thriller" dance, moonwalk and all, while the lions just sat there staring at him.

When he walked out of that lion's pit the next day, all I could do was just throw up my hands and shake my head.

"What type of extraterrestrial world do you live in when the lions don't bite?"

Edward was the same way! Just cool as a cucumber no matter what the circumstances were. It was frustrating because I tried to have his head blown off many times for being a good Christian, but God always found a way to protect him.

No matter how daunting of a task given to him by the pastor, Edward always made a success out of it, or at least tried.

Frank was curious why his father was treated so poorly by the pastor, and it pissed him off. His father was out at all times of the night, hustling up members for the small church. And the pastor and first lady would reap all the benefits.

That's why he was so excited when his father decided to leave the small Pentecostal church and start his own. Edward never told Frank exactly why he chose to leave Vine Street Pentecostal Church, but

Frank assumed that his father just got tired of being pissed on by the pastor.

Edward took great pride in being a minister, and he made sure that that message was relayed to the world through his family. When Frank looked into the eyes of his parents, he saw a righteous woman who was proud to be with a righteous man. But they struggled financially.

A tiny white shotgun house on Myrtle Avenue was all that the family could afford, but at times it was embarrassing for Frank. The front door opened to the living room, then Frank's room, his parent's room, a kitchen, and the bathroom. No hallways, just flimsy doors separating rooms. Frank always had to have clothing near, or risk being caught naked when a visitor walked through his room to get to the bathroom.

Another eyesore for the family, which would be my focus, was the family's transportation. It was agonizing for Edward to pull up to the church in a rusted-out, 86 Chevy Caprice Estate Wagon, while the pastor switched out Cadillacs like socks.

Frank could see the contempt in his father's eyes as Pastor Ford and the first family pulled up in the latest, limited-edition Cadillac, while his rusted out, bucket of bolts would convulse and shake like it was afraid to turn off.

Pastor Ford would slide out of his shiny new car and look at Edward and his family as if he were disgusted.

"Brother Edward, can I have a world with you. Brother Edward, I love you! But that car is spilling oil all over the street in front of the church. Is there any way you can pull that thing around to the back alley and park? We want our church to represent the cleanliness of Christ, and that car is just a rusty, unclean, eyesore."

Edward would smile and try to ignore the comment, but the embarrassment was painful for him.

An embarrassment to you is also a big tool I often use to fight for souls with God! The feeling of embarrassment can be a shock to anyone, especially when there is absolutely nothing you can do about it.

I couldn't have Edward let the embarrassment slide, so I start pushing buttons. I needed him first to feel shameful and then move him towards depression. The best way to accomplish that goal is to involve his wife and child in it.

"How can you call yourself a man? This man just called you a bum in front of your wife and son. And all you can do is stand there with that goofy-ass smile on your face. You're looking like a real lame-ass right now! How can you be a real man if you let another man disrespect you in front of your wife and son?"

Edward tried to ignore me, but I'm relentless. You might not pay attention to me at that moment, but I guarantee that you'll say yes to the right circumstances. And that's all I do! I create circumstances that bend your reality to benefit me.

All the pastor's cars were leased through the church. Also, his house loan was paid directly through the church. And all his wife's weekly spa visits were paid by church tithes.

Church tithes from church members whom Edward had convinced to come join in the first place. It had to be very disheartening as a father to have your wife and son wearing clothes from the Salvation Army, while the first family wore the latest fashions from Macy's and Saks Fifth Avenue.

Edward Barkley leaving Vine St. Pentecostal would be Armageddon for Pastor Ford and his family. The foundation that stabilized Vine St. Pentecostal was basically being pulled out from under them. Pastor Ford may have received all the financial benefits, but Edward was the person that people came to see.

Edward had tried to move forward from the embarrassment of the car comment, but I paralyzed him with shame.

Anytime I saw him pick up the bible and try to clear his mind, I would start talking to him.

"How's that supposed to help you? You slave at that stinking barrel company sometimes twelve and thirteen hours a day and you still don't have anything to show. Your wife and son wear hand-me-down clothes, and that shotgun shack that you call a house is falling around you. Any man that can't provide the basic needs for his family is not fit to be called a Man. Are you disabled?! Are you handicapped?! Then what the fuck is your excuse? You do God's will day and night, and you can't even provide for your wife and kid. Look at your wife? She's young and beautiful! Why in God's name would she stay with you? I bet if Pastor Ford were in your predicament, he would most certainly do something about it."

I know I hurt Edward's feelings, but sometimes being hurt makes you resourceful. You start thinking about what's most important in your life. And make no doubt about it, his family was the most important part of his life, especially his wife, Mariyah.

Frank's mother had a beautiful soul, but she had given up a lot to be with Edward.

Frank's mother was born in a small town in Kentucky. Growing up in a small town only allowed you small-town dreams, and Mariyah wanted more. When she became a teenager, she avoided all the trappings of the small town.

Hanging with the fast girls over by the railroad tracks and getting pregnant was the easiest way of throwing your life away and getting stuck at the clothing factory. Every summer, Mariyah left the small town and headed to Cincinnati to stay with her cousins. Everything about Cincinnati was just bigger and livelier. Her dream was to graduate Nursing School in Cincinnati, and she was well on her away to achieving that dream. She saved her money and finally moved to Cincinnati permanently. She enrolled in Nursing School to fulfill her goal, and then a friendly janitor named Edward derailed her aspirations.

Mariyah's goals did not evaporate overnight; they just slowly faded away as Edward and she got closer.

Edward was light-skinned and he stood about six feet four inches. He had broad shoulders, and his brown eyes brightened when he spoke, loud and boisterous, but Mariyah's virgin curiosity was attracted to his confidence.

Edward was also attracted to Mariyah. She had short dark hair, big brown eyes and bronze skin. She would lean forward and bashfully cover her bright smile when he told his corny jokes. Edward would only try harder to be a comedian when he saw the huge grin spread across her face, forming two deep dimples in her cheeks.

There was nothing special about Edward to the naked eye. He was not wealthy, and in fact, had dropped out of school in the 10th grade. But Mariyah saw those intangible qualities in him that would make him special.

The church became the glue that held them together. Mariyah's parents objected to the marriage because they saw how the relationship was affecting her goals. She took the NCLEX exam twice and failed. Not because she didn't know the material, but because her mind was preoccupied.

Getting married, having sex for the first time, and getting pregnant has a way of preoccupying anyone's thoughts.

As her dreams of becoming a registered nurse slowly began to fade away, she became inspired by Edward's potential. He accepted Christ into his life and was called to preach within a year. But becoming a minister also had negative implications on his relationship with his family.

Edward's family had never really accepted Mariyah because she had taken Edward away from them. Not physically or mentally, but spiritually. The once loud and boisterous Edward, who would drink excessively and play cards at his mother's house, simply disappeared one day. The family blamed Mariyah but in actuality, Edward had changed his life because of Christ. Edward still visited with his family, but only when the alcohol and other transgressions of his faith were not present.

Mariyah tried to be friendly towards his family, but she was met with cold stares and whispers. She felt out of place when Edward and his family would reminisce about all the alcohol-fueled parties. She felt more comfortable alone at the small house on Myrtle avenue, listening to gospel music with little Frank. She knew Edward's mother disliked her, but she also began to see signs of her hatred slowly turning towards Frank. The straw that broke the camel's back for her happened on Christmas day.

She allowed Frank to stay overnight with his cousins for the Christmas Eve gathering. The annual gathering was huge for Edward's family because all of the children received presents from aunts and uncles. But the nicest gifts came from Edward's mother. Grandma Melba would save money all year long just to shower her grandchildren with gifts.

Edward had cautioned Mariyah to tamper her expectations, but Mariyah was just so excited about finally having Frank included in something with his cousins. She was appalled when she arrived on Christmas day and saw Frank in the corner alone playing with one of his cousin's old Stretch Armstrong dolls, while his cousins gleefully darted back and forth outside on new bikes.

Edward admonished his family, and his mother offered to buy Frank a new bike. But in Mariyah's mind, the damage had already been done. Edward had become excluded by his family, and Mariyah and Frank were collateral damage.

As I stated before, there was nothing special about Edward. But Mariyah cultivated those intangible qualities of a leader in him, and that would make him special.

He had a passion and drive. No matter how many times he failed, he had the grit and determination to keep going after what he wanted. And the most important trait about Edward was that he was resourceful.

Edward did everything he could to ignore me, but reality is the greatest teacher. You may wrap yourself in a cocoon of spirituality and close your eyes about what I say, but I control everyday experiences, not Christ.

Being broke on your own and being broke in a relationship are two different animals. When you're broke on your own, you don't feel like your financial status is bringing anyone down. In fact, you can do a decent job of hiding your financial status. You can't hide your money problems when you're married with a child, and you're both struggling financially.

Edward felt ashamed of not fulfilling his financial obligations to his family, and he judged himself as weak. He and Mariyah tried hard to stay under the radar and hide their financial problems, but it was obvious that they were struggling. Edward would borrow money from family members or rob Peter to pay Paul.

There were people in the church who offered to support Edward if he decided to start a church. And there were even times that he gave it serious consideration.

Edward heard the comments when he preached at guest churches. Church leaders would pull Pastor Ford to the side and whisper.

"You better take good care of him, because he's going to be a big fish."

Instead of sharing those occasions with the star of his team, Pastor Ford used those opportunities to gain special financial attention from the hosting church. There were even rumors that Pastor Ford was charging an appearance fee for Edward and pocketing the fee.

Edward was curious about the financial side because, after all, Pastor Ford was taking home a nice piece of change.

Vine Street Pentecostal Church was small, but it was bringing in just over $100,000 per year. $60,000 of that budget was going into Pastor Ford's pocket. In other words, Pastor ford was receiving 6 of every 10 dollars that entered the storehouse.

And your star player's salary, non-existent!

Can you imagine that?

The Chicago Bulls win seven championships, and Michael Jordan does not get a penny?!

But hey, who am I to judge!

Edward was uncompromising in his belief that a man profits nothing if he gains the whole world yet loses his own soul. Edward just wanted to teach God's word and bring in as many souls as possible.

So, what did he do? He ignored the chatter.

To him, it would have been less than genuine to listen to that type of talk, when he was loyal to the pastor.

He didn't entertain the thought until I gave him a reason to listen, and that occurred one hot and muggy Easter Sunday.

The morning started bad because the Chevy wagon's radiator finally blew up. Edward had sealed and re-sealed the radiator so many times, that the seats inside the car smelled like the sealant. That Sunday, it simply blew up for the final time.

Easter Sunday was a big deal at Vine St. Pentecostal, and Edward Barkley was the main attraction.

Being a dedicated minister, he had called everyone, including the pastor, to see if he could get a ride to church.

No matter how many people he called, no one seemed available, or the short notice was an issue. Edward understood people's routines on Easter Sunday. You attended Sunrise service at 6 am and went home to get ready for the big show at 11 am. Sunrise service was not even on Edward's radar; he just wanted to be on time for the 11 am service.

When he called Pastor Ford's phone, he figured that he was screening calls in the church study, because the phone rang a couple of times and went to voicemail. Ordinarily, it would not have been a big deal, but today Edward really needed his help.

I didn't make the situation any easier for him. My goal is to push you to the limit, and sweet Jesus was I going to press Edward.

You can cry out to Christ for help, but I swear your life will never be the same when I'm finished.

Edward called the pastor's number, hoping that he would see it was an emergency, but no one answered.

I saw the pitiful expression on his face and started talking.

"That's who you give your loyalty. Pastor Ford is sitting in his air-conditioned church study, eating breakfast, and watching a brand-new color TV. You haven't even eaten breakfast yet because you've been trying to bum a ride from the good saints at Vine Street Pentecostal. You're hot and sweaty, and your hands are covered with engine grease. Look at your wife and kid pacing back in forth in their new Easter clothes from Goodwill, and all you can do is shake your head in frustration. You're not a man! You're not even half-a-man! Your wife makes more money than you."

It was a low blow, but I was just presenting him with his reality. He had to work a double shift just to make half of what Mariyah was making as a nursing assistant.

Edward left a frantic voice message, practically begging Pastor Ford for help.

Edward lowered the phone back to the receiver and placed his sweaty face in the palm of his hand. He leaned back in the chair and growled loudly.

"God, what else can go wrong?"

I smiled to myself and shook my head.

"Well Mr.' I'm going to serve God to my dying day'! You're about to find out!"

After waiting for an hour and a half without a response, Edward decided that the family would just have to ride the bus. The metro bus always ran behind schedule on Sundays, so the family was already running late. When they finally arrived at church, it was almost 11:45 am, and people were testifying. Edward tried to enter the church quietly, but the unoiled door hinges shrieked like a terrified girl in a horror picture.

Edward sat in the rear of the church with his family and waited patiently. Pastor Ford glared at Edward as if being late was the ultimate sin. Edward quickly glanced in another direction because he was already hot and frustrated.

The pastor motioned to an usher and pointed in Edward's direction. The usher walked over to Edward and gave his elbow a slight tug. Pastor Ford wanted Edward escorted to the pulpit in the middle of testimony service, and Edward felt obligated to follow. He was upset with the pastor but not to the point of making a scene in God's house. Pastor Ford embraced Edward and pretended to catch the spirit by quickly jerking his body from side to side and screaming.

"Yes Lord! Thank you, Lord! I can feel the anointing, yes lord."

The pastor continued to sway back and forth with Edward in his arms as he started to moan and speak in a harmonized-melody.

"Hallelujah! Hallelujah! Whatever you want, you can get it. Whatever you need, God's got it."

Edward's stomach rumbled like a train track as he noticed the smell of bacon and fresh griddled cakes seeping from Pastor Ford's suit.

I would not be Satan if I allowed that to go unnoticed.

"You see what I'm saying? This dirty motherfucker has been tossing back flapjacks and bacon all morning, while you and your family missed breakfast to ride the Metro. I mean really Edward?! Not to be too sarcastic, but your pastor really cares about you."

The organ began to vibrate through the small church as the crowd went into a feverish sing-along, call and response with Pastor Ford.

"He's got every."

Every!

Every!

Every!

"Everything that you will need."

The crowd quickly broke into a frenzy dance, as the beat of the drum kept time with the organ.

Pastor Ford's embrace of Edward suddenly released, and he extended his hands toward Edward and grabbed both wrists. He rocked back and forth with uncontrollable laughter as if he were Ray Charles. His large head tilted backward, and a single gold tooth glimmered in the sun. He banged his large fat hand against Edward's back and moved him toward the rostrum. The pastor let out a wild, tribal scream and lifted Edward's arm in the air as if they were campaigning for re-election.

Pastor Ford motioned for Edward to step back, and he began to speak.

"God has blessed us in so many ways since last Easter that we can't even start to be thankful."

People in the audience shook their heads in agreement as the pastor continued speaking.

"When God is blessing you, it's important to pay that blessing forward. And this morning, God has placed it on my heart to pay a blessing forward. God wants me to give a special person in this church ten thousand dollars."

The crowd shot out of their seats and applauded loudly as the pastor glanced in Edward's direction and winked.

For a split second, Edward felt like God was going to answer his prayer. Ten thousand dollars could go a long way in Edward's house. He could buy a good used car for five thousand dollars, pay off the rest of the CG&E bill, and put a little bit towards Frank's school tuition. The Sisters at St. Francis de Sales School were probably tired of hearing his sad stories about only having partial tuition again.

The thought of finally getting a little financial break brought a smile to Edward's face as he counted all the possibilities of having ten thousand dollars.

Edward held both hands in the air and hollered at the top of his lungs.

"Amen! Thank you, Jesus, Bless us Lord."

Pastor Ford looked back at Edward and rolled his eyes as if annoyed that he had been interrupted. He turned back toward the congregation and continued talking.

"This brother has always been here struggling with us, even when we only had fifty members. And now that we have grown to two hundred and fifty members, he is still right here sacrificing with us."

Edward looked out at the congregation and saw smiles in all directions. He didn't want the congregation to have any type of hatred toward him, because he probably would have felt guilty about accepting the ten thousand dollars. Seeing their smiling faces reassured him that this was a blessing from God.

Again, Edward held his hands high in the air nearly crying, as he praised God.

"Yes Lord, thank you, heavenly father for your blessings."

No one in the church deserved that check more than Edward, because he had literally sacrificed everything to do God's work.

As an enemy of Christ, it never made sense to me when a person sacrificed everything including his self-dignity and family, for a few brownie points with God.

Edward literally took his cross up to follow God. The congregation saw how he sacrificed wealth, reputation, comfort, and convenience just to do God's will at Vine Street Pentecostal.

Pastor Ford waved the check in the air like he had just won a gold medal at the Olympics.

He stepped back and admired the congregation as the anticipation grew, and then he leaned his body toward the microphone and almost screamed.

"Come on up here Chunky and get this check."

There was an immediate state of shock in the congregation, which elicited loud gasps and sighs of disappointment from several people.

No one in the church was expecting to hear Chunky Henderson's name.

Chunky Henderson owned Chunky's Barbeque, a small hole-in-the-wall that offered generous portions of rib tips. You could literally feed the whole family with one plate. There would be so many rib tips slathered in spicy barbeque, that you couldn't even close the lid of the styrofoam tray. The line would stretch out the door, and you would have to fight the mosquitoes and giant flies. A loudspeaker mounted in the corner would crackle as it pumped out old school sounds from WCIN. Chunky had made a lot of money off that little shit-hole of a restaurant, and now the pastor was endowing him with an extra ten thousand dollars.

Chunky slowly zig-zagged toward the front of the church and fell into the outstretched arms of Pastor Ford.

"Brotha, Brotha, you shouldn't have."

He reminded Edward of Congressman Lincoln from the movie, Uptown Saturday Night. His voice was loud and boisterous, and he spoke in a low, contrite tone. His accent reminded him of a dusty old Englishman.

Pastor Ford and Chunky Henderson whispered back and forth into each other's ears and laughed, as if they were the only ones who got the joke.

The sound of the crowd's disgruntled moans was drowned out by Pastor Ford's wife banging away on the old Hammond B3 organ, connected to the single 122 Leslie speaker.

Edward's face went numb as the name Chunky reverberated through the giant speaker hanging from the wall. It was like everything was happening in slow motion as the pastor embraced Chunky like a long lost brother. His sense of time departed as the surreal sound of white noise echoed in his ears as Pastor Ford silenced the music and continued to talk.

"We have never really taken time to thank Chunky Henderson for always giving this church great barbeque, and in some cases, free barbeque. Chunky called me on the phone this morning and told me that God had given him a vision. Do you want to know what that vision was?"

Edward glared at the short, portly pastor with the jheri curl. Tiny beads of sweat mixed with curl activator made his head glisten like Soul Glow Darryl.

The audience gave a half-hearted amen in response to his question and the pastor countered with an eerie tormented laugh, which reminded Edward of Dr. Evil from those Austin Powers movies.

Chunky took a step back from the podium and nudged Edward slightly to the side as Pastor Ford continued to talk.

"God has told Chunky that a food truck will be a blessing not only to this community but also to this church, and God placed it in my heart to give him ten thousand dollars."

Pastor Ford leaned slightly forward over the rostrum and stared at the audience, unmoving as if they should be ecstatic because they were witnessing a miracle.

The expressions writing across the faces of some of Pastor Ford's most loyal members spoke volumes about his decision to go public with this announcement. He quickly glanced over at Edward and raised his arm. His chubby hand began to move like he was directing a puppet, as he motioned Edward forward.

Edward slanted his head to one side and glared at Pastor Ford for a long moment and then moved toward the podium. Pastor Ford's portly body sashayed toward Chunky and draped his arm around his neck, as if they were posing for a best friend's edition of GQ magazine.

Edward slowly removed the microphone from the stand, and deliberately stalled by untangling the long cord as if he were roping cattle with a lasso. The uneasy silence caused a nervous murmur to spread through the crowd, as they tried to guess Edward's next move.

Pastor Ford finally noticed the anxious audience and winked at them. He stepped behind Edward and playfully poked him in the small of his back with his finger.

"Come on doc, I know you have something to say. You always have something uplifting to say."

Pastor Ford returned to his spot near Chunky and flashed a mischievous smile. The smile evoked something within Edward that he had never felt before. The cars, home, jewelry, and now the cash give away, made his skin cringe with jealously.

Edward looked toward the rear of the church and saw his wife holding Frank closely. She had sacrificed everything to be the perfect wife, and all he could give his family was a two-bedroom shotgun house, a broken-down Chevy station wagon, and a pile of bills.

Edward's thoughts were briefly sidetracked when Pastor Ford leaned forward and whispered in his ear.

Come on, Brother Barkley! You have to speed this part of the service up because we have to get to the offering. Just give a quick testimony, and let's get these plates passed around. There are too many people here today to be trying to save souls. We have to get that money baby! Get that money."

Edward smiled at Pastor Ford, but his eyes were full of rage. In his mind, he was saying:

"Really, you want me to testify about the goodness of God when I'm contemplating if I should beat the shit out of you."

The anger in Edward's eyes was enough to make Pastor Ford retreat to the safety of his spot near Chunky, but the congregation noticed the tension.

Some members showed their disgust by standing up and walking out of the church.

"He knows that he was wrong for that! Elder Barkley has been coming to this church faithfully and never asked for a dime. This man is catching the bus to church, and you giving money to somebody who's got three cars, the nerve of some people."

The silly grin on Pastor Ford's face made him look like a child caught with his hand in the cookie jar. He tried to curb the insurgence amongst church members by snatching the microphone from Edward.

"Hey, hey, people, hold on for a minute. Yawl didn't let me finish with what else God wanted me to do. God also placed it in my heart to get brother Barkley's car fixed. God placed it on my heart, right after I found out about his situation from Deacon Pool this morning."

Deacon Pool sprang out of his seat in the front pew, almost falling forward on his face.

"Now that's a lie! Don't try and bring me into this mess."

Deacon Pool was a short, middle-aged guy with a loud, raspy voice. The bright sun bounced off his balding head, as he spilled the beans about the magnitude of Pastor Ford's deceitfulness.

"You told me that Elder Barkley left a message looking for a ride because his car broke down. And your exact words were, "that's his fault, because he should have bought another car." And I didn't find out how bad the situation was until after Sunday school."

Deacon Pool looked around the church frantically, finally finding his wife and pointing, as if he were a super sleuth having an aha! moment."

"Didn't he, Ella? And what did he say when brother Barkley and his family walked in?"

Deacon Pool never gave his wife a chance to respond because he answered his own question.

'He said I guess brother Barkley found a way to church after all. It's funny how God works if you solve your own problems."

Deacon Pool nodded his large shiny head up and down.

Mmm-hum that's exactly what you said! No sir Pastor, I'm not getting involved in this. This is your problem."

Deacon Pool looked around the room and nodded his head, searching to see if anyone agreed with him.

Half of the crowd stared at Pastor Ford in dismay, wondering why a man of God could be so cruel to a person who had sacrificed so much to Vine Street Pentecostal Church.

Had Edward done something to fall out of favor with Pastor Ford, and he was punishing him out. Or was this something personal, and the church was getting the backend of the story.

The other half of the congregation waited impatiently for Edward's rebuttal. This had been a long time coming. Half the people in the church were fed up with the way Edward was being taken advantage of. Most of the younger members in the church were saved because of Edward's teachings. Although Christ was in them, they were brash and full of youthful energy. They were still learning how to walk a righteous path and sometimes reverted back to the old way of handling conflict. This was one of those situations.

A lot of people expected Edward to curse Pastor Ford out and walk out of the church, but that was not who Edward was. Going crazy in the pulpit would have shown those young saints in the church that he couldn't handle conflict. Besides, that was the opposite of who he was. Edward had a kind, gentle heart beneath his rough and tough exterior.

Most women, and some of the men, thought that Edward's tall slender body with light skin was attractive. But there were other people like Pastor Ford, who only saw Edward as a light, bright, and damn near white-skinned pretty boy.

Pastor Ford tried to regain control of Deacon Pool and the church by quoting a series of bible verses that made absolutely no sense.

"The one sinless among you let him cast the first stone. Judge not, that ye be not judged. For with what judgment ye judge, ye shall be judged; and with what measure ye mete, it shall be measured to you again. And why beholdest thou the mote that is in thy brother's eye, but considerest not the beam that is in thine own eye?"

Most of the church stared at Pastor Ford in shock as he fumbled through the bible, looking for more bible verses to quote.

The crowd reacted like they were watching a professional curler describing why he should be on the same level as Lebron James.

Exactly! Nobody cared about his explanation.

People were tired of Pastor Ford, and some of the younger saints expressed how they felt by trolling Pastor Ford and making a Pac-Man dying sound.

"error dok dok."

A line of people was waiting to exit the small Church when Edward's soft, silky voice interrupted the flow of the disgruntled church members.

"Good morning saints!"

The dissenting crowd stopped moving and turned toward the pulpit as Edward continued.

"Saints, first I want to apologize to everyone in this Church because I came to Church in the wrong spirit. As I've been standing here watching all the events unfold today, I'm reminded of second Corinthians 1:3-4. Paul talked about how suffering is useful in comforting and helping others."

The audience responded in unity and agreement.

"Amen Elder, you better teach that word."

Edward's voice grew clearer and more passionate as the cheap wall speakers rattled with the richness of his voice.

"Blessed be the God and Father of our Lord Jesus Christ, the Father of mercies and God of all comfort, who comforts us in all of our affliction, so that we may be able to comfort those who are in any affliction, with the comfort with which we ourselves are comforted by God."

Amen saints. This is not something we should take lightly. Instead of rejoicing about my car breaking down, I was upset because no one responded. And instead of me rejoicing about brother Chunky being blessed, I became discouraged because I felt that should have been me."

Pastor Ford came to life and roared like a wild boar, as he strutted across the stage like an out of control peacock.

Amen! That's right! You have to be satisfied with what you got before God blesses you."

Edward glanced at Pastor Ford as if annoyed by his antics and continued to speak.

"God often uses our most difficult struggles to help others with similar struggles. A person who has struggled with an eating disorder is often the best person to help someone else with this struggle. A former alcoholic is often the best counselor to others seeking to break from the control of alcohol. While these trials are not enjoyable, God can and does use our weaknesses to bring hope to others."

Pastor Ford appeared to catch the spirit and started speaking in tongues. He looked like a short, bald, alcoholic staggering around the pulpit speaking incoherently. His fictitious walk on the spiritual side quickly came to a halt as Edward continued.

"Trials also remind us that something better lies ahead for those who believe. In Romans 8:18 Paul wrote, 'For I consider that the sufferings of this present time are not worth comparing with the glory that is to be revealed to us.' Though he faced many difficulties, he knew they could be endured because he knew something far greater awaited him."

Edward turned toward Pastor Ford, who by now had given Edward his full attention.

"Pastor Ford, I thank you for allowing me to grow into the man I am today. We didn't always see eye to eye, but nevertheless, you have been my spiritual father. When I had no direction or purpose for my life, I found it here at Vine Street Pentecostal Church. But there comes a time in every boy's life when he must become a man.

"Colossians 3:21 says fathers do not provoke your children to anger but bring them up in the discipline and instruction of the Lord."

Edward held his hand up and pointed towards his wife and Frank. The entire Church turned slowly towards Edward's wife and son.

"You know, saints, sometimes I have to discipline my son Frank; it hurts me to discipline him but there are times when I have no choice. There used to be a time when I had little or no patience, and spanked Frank for the smallest infractions."

Edward then turned towards Pastor Ford and held his hand in his direction.

"There were also times that Pastor Ford had to discipline me spiritually, but there have also been times when I felt the discipline was not needed. Parents can cause their children to become angry and bitter. I'm sure you know this, and I can assure you that they know this. But I think we can go even a step further to say there are times when our children are justified in their anger toward us. There are times when we so provoke our children; we so exasperate them, that anger is the fitting response. It may even be the right response if that anger is expressed righteously. There may be times when your children's anger toward you is more righteous than your actions or attitude toward them.

A discouraged child is one who has lost heart. He is so beaten down that he has lost hope, he has lost motivation, and he doesn't care anymore. The Bible translates it, 'lest he gets discouraged and quit trying.' The idea here is that you can beat down your children so that they stop trying to please you. Maybe your demands are arbitrary or unfair. Maybe you never praise your children and take joy in them. Perhaps you live hypocritically before them with higher expectations for them than for yourself. Whatever the case, they eventually stop caring and stop trying. In this Bible verse, we see that Paul does not want to see the children of Christian families disciplined to such an extent that they lose heart and simply give up trying to please their parents."

Edward glanced back at Pastor Ford, with tears in his eyes. The betrayal and disappointment were etched in his features. He looked into Pastor Ford's eyes but didn't seem to be looking at him. It was more like he was looking through him.

And with one final breath, he stunned the entire congregation at Vine St. Pentecostal Church.

"In other words, I no longer need or want your guidance, because today, I have become a man. Pastor Ford, I wish you nothing but the best. But the Bible says, 'Watch the path of your feet, and all your ways will be established.' I think it's time that I establish my own path for Christ and walk it, blessed Pastor."

You could literally hear a pin drop as he stepped out of the pulpit and made his way towards the door. Frank and Mariyah met Edward just as he was exiting the door, which made his departure look almost presidential. Some members were applauding while others cried and followed behind him.

When Edward left Vine St. Pentecostal, it literally became a walk of faith for the family. Edward had no idea where he was going spiritually. Pastor Ford recommended the ultimate penalty for Edward, which was to be silenced for ninety days. After ninety days, he was expected to give a public apology during the church service or be banned;

Edward chose banishment. Edward could not see himself apologizing to the person who treated him like a steppingstone. Edward believed that he and his family should have been treated better, and he walked away embarrassed, feeling like discarded trash.

Word of Edward's departure from Vine St. Pentecostal Church, became like open recruitment for his services. St. Paul Methodist, First Corinthian Baptist, St. Stephens Episcopal, and the list went on and on. It was like a five- star athlete announcing that he was leaving his first choice, and other schools were clamoring for his services. All of these churches requesting his services had heard about his ability to electrify the audience with his auditory presence or seen it personally.

Edward had a unique ability to tap into a person's image concept, discard the negative, and make them feel special regardless of their circumstances. All these organizations wanted Edward to come in and reignite their church members' fire, but none of these organizations were willing to allow him to be the Pastor.

Most of the churches in Cincinnati, including the ones courting Edward, wanted the big, bright, pretty fire, to remain in their camp. In other words, they wanted Edward to only cater to people in their territory or people associated with their territory.

The territorial church lines had been established in Cincinnati, in the mid-eighties. For example, if you were a member of St. Paul Methodist Church, you damn sure didn't attend St. Stephens Baptist, even if it was just for a visit. You had to get permission from both pastors involved, and above all, it was about respecting church territory.

Pastors would meet and carve up a main thoroughfare like Vine Street and claim the territory. The larger churches would get the most territory, while the smaller churches were squeezed out. Churches were extremely possessive of their territories, and that's why Edward was perceived as an ally or enemy.

Most of the churches in Cincinnati viewed Edward as a spiritual poacher. He never spoke with people to intentionally try and steer them to Vine Street Pentecostal, it was just something about what he said that left you craving for more.

First Corinthian Baptist Church would be facing financial disaster if Edward joined St. Paul Methodist.

All it took was a hired poacher like Edward to cross territories and tip the scales one way or the other. It was vitally important that all these churches reach deep into their coffers and come up with the best financial package to offer Edward.

Two thousand dollars, weekly car rentals, and a six-month mortgage deal was the standard rate for an above-average minister like Edward. Edward probably could have negotiated for more, but he was just tired of the servitude. Depending on another man's scrapings to support his family was no longer in his vocabulary. He had never attended college, but he knew the type of money he was bringing in for Pastor Ford.

Edward had been happily teaching the word of God. He didn't care about the money—all that changed after Easter Sunday because he was curious about being financially stable.

Had Pastor Ford simply broken bread with him on that Sunday, nothing would have changed. He would still be in the middle of Linn Street, screaming about how much Jesus loves them, broke as a joke.

That Easter Sunday was an eye-opener for Edward. It was like Eve taking that first bite of the tree of knowledge and finding a new perspective. He made more money being a guest evangelist at different churches, then being the star attraction at Vine Street Pentecostal

The offers continued to flood the Barkley household, but Edward was in no rush to join anyone's Church after the betrayal he had just gone through.

No offer really had his full attention until Brother Askew knocked on his door three months later.

Brother Askew was not your normal 'follow the rules' type of Christian. He came to Church periodically, but no one considered him a bible thumper. He was the type of person who seemed to come to Church just to feel good, but he stayed away from the politics.

Edward had spoken to Brother Askew a couple of times at Vine Street Pentecostal church, but it was nothing formal. Pastor Ford had once warned him about Brother Askew being uppity because he had attended law school.

Edward was surprised to see Brother Askew, and it showed when he greeted him with caution and uncertainty.

"Hey, how's it going?"

Brother Askew responded with a loud, vibrant reply.

"Good afternoon Elder Barkley. I'm not sure if you remember me, but I'm Brother Askew, Brother Travis Askew. I saw you preach at Vine Street Pentecostal a few times."

Edward narrowed his eyes as if he were having a hard time focusing, and then jerked his head toward the ceiling as if he had just had an epiphany.

"Oh yes! I do remember you Brother Askew, come on in."

Edward fumbled with the lock and opened the tattered screen door. He smiled and held his hand out, and Brother Askew lunged forward, gripping Edward in a paralyzing bear hug.

"It's so good to see you Elder Barkley."

Edward quickly bounced his hand up and down on Travis' back and slowly pulled away from his embrace.

Travis smiled and continued to hold Edward's hand, and rested his other hand on Edward's shoulder as his tone became more serious.

"Elder Barkley, I don't mean to impose on you and your family, but I've been trying to get in contact with you. I just wanted to tell you that most of the members at Vine Street Pentecostal felt that you were treated unfairly on Easter Sunday. That speech you gave pretty much summed up how we were all feeling, at least my family and me."

Edward shook his head in approval and his forehead crinkled in concern as Travis changed the subject.

"Speaking of family, I just wanted you to know that my parents have been big fans of yours since the first time they heard you speak. They taped you on a VHS film and they must have played that thing almost every day. More importantly, they want you to consider an offer to be a Senior Pastor."

The concern on Edward's face turned into a surprised look seeking more information.

"Oh really, I'm flattered, but I can't quite place your parents. Did I ever visit their Church?"

Travis shook his head in disagreement.

"No! My parents live in Atlanta, Georgia. They came up here a couple times when I was still attending the University of Cincinnati. It's funny because I found Vine Street Pentecostal by accident."

Edward motioned for Travis to sit down and Travis thanked him.

"Elder Barkley, you may not remember, but you invited me to that Church when you came on campus one time. I was stressed about passing the bar exam, and you stopped me as I was on my way to my dorm. It was like you saw the hurt in me and asked me if I needed prayer. When you prayed for me, it was like everything felt better. It was like a fifty-pound weight was taken off my shoulder. When I got to my dorm room, I received notification that I passed. When I called my mother and told her what had happened, she told me that it had to be God. I came to the Church a couple of times because I wanted to tell my testimony, but the timing was always wrong. I mean, there were so many people at the Church with testimonies in far worse situations. I couldn't exactly testify about passing the bar exam when people were being saved from drug abuse and surviving life-threatening injuries.

Edward shook his head in agreement and laughed.

"I can certainly understand that Brother Travis, but God knows your heart."

Travis smiled, and then the tone of his voice lowered as if he were telling Edward a top secret.

"You know, my parents were at Church that Sunday you left. Both my parents believe that it was a blessing in disguise, because you deserve so much better. My father has been calling me almost daily trying to see if I made contact with you. He wants you to pastor his Church in Atlanta."

Edward leaned back and rested his elbows on the chair's armrest and folded his hands over his chest.

"I don't know about that, Travis! Atlanta is seven or eight hours away from Cincinnati. I'd probably worry myself to death driving back and forth. You know, with my family and all."

Travis held his hand out as if conducting a traffic stop.

"No, no, no. I think you're misunderstanding what I'm asking. My father's not asking you to drive back and forth, his asking you to move to Atlanta permanently."

Travis opened a weathered, black-leather bag, and fished out a large, bulky, manila clasp envelope. He placed the large envelope on the wobbly coffee table, and the table nearly collapsed from the weight. Travis studied Edward's facial expression as he slowly pushed the envelope in his direction.

Edward glanced at the large envelope and swallowed hard. He had seen that type of envelope exchange hands many times before at

Church. He could almost eyeball the amount because he was a deacon for eight years. He had only seen that size of envelope and contents during the last day of a General Assembly.

Every member of the Church was required to give money to the Bishop, the amount depended on your title. Pastors, Elders, Ministers, and Mothers in the Church were required to give one hundred dollars, while regular church members had to pony up twenty-five to fifty dollars. Edward and the other deacons would take the large white buckets, filled with money to the basement. The crumpled bills would get straightened enough for presentation and folded into thousand-dollar bundles.

Oh yes! Edward had seen that type of envelope before.

Edward picked the large envelope up and carefully examined the outside. The thickness, the size, and the weight, Edward estimated that the envelope held approximately five to eight thousand dollars.

Travis smiled at Edward and continued the conversation.

That's for you, Elder Barkley. We understand that the move to Atlanta might be a little rough on the family. So, we wanted to come up with something to try and help lighten that burden. It's not a lot, but my parents wanted to give you something that shows that they are interested in having you as their Pastor."

Edward gently tossed the envelope up and down and responded.

"Travis look, I'm really flattered by your offer, but I don't think I'm right for your parents' Church. I helped build Vine Street Pentecostal from a twelve-member storefront church to well over three hundred members. I just don't think I have the energy to do that all over again."

If I'm going to pastor a church, I want something already established. It's just not worth moving to Atlanta and trying to rebuild another storefront church."

Travis' face twitched as he moved his head backward like he was dodging a flying object and laughed.

"Elder Barkley, I think you have the wrong idea about my parents' Church. Solid Foundation Cathedral is far from a dingy storefront church. Solid Foundation Cathedral has over 5,000 members listed on the books, with at least 2,500 of those members attending regularly every Sunday. I'm not sending you to a pit of despair; in fact, it could be quite prosperous for you and your family. Solid Foundation already has a solid tithing base as well as a community willing to support the right person. This could be a special opportunity for you if you're willing to step out on faith."

Edward had heard about Atlanta, Georgia, but he never really envisioned himself moving there until he opened the envelope. Edward ripped the seal of the envelope apart, just as the living room door opened.

Frank came to the living room door and introduced himself to Travis.

Travis responded with a bright smile and an overly friendly voice, "Good afternoon young man!"

He glanced in Edward's direction and saw him looking back and forth at Travis and then at the contents of the envelope. His face was fixated with an intense gaze as if he were holding his breath.

He walked over to Edward and gently rubbed his back.

"Is everything ok, Dad?

Frank glanced over Edward's shoulder and saw an envelope stuffed with several stacks of hundred-dollar bills, wrapped in rubber bands. The expression on his face was blended with shock and surprise.

Edward tilted his head upwards toward his son's face and smiled.

"Everything is fine, son. I believe everything is going to be just fine."

Entry:
Frank's Enlightenment

Edward and Frank may have been tempted differently, but the end result is always the same; you can't serve two masters. Edward had to either find a way to deal with being poor and serving Christ or revise what he believed. I don't care how strong you think you are in your faith. When I toss those money bags in your direction, it'll change your whole thought process. Ask Osteen, Hinn, Dollar, or Myers. I'll have you backtracking every Sunday just to stay in that position, and Edward Barkley was no different.

The move from Cincinnati to Atlanta was like a breath of fresh air for Frank and the family. Frank was excited because he enjoyed the city life. And compared to Cincinnati, Atlanta was double the size. His mother worried about how the move to Atlanta would affect her family financially. Could they afford a nice home in a safe neighborhood? What about Frank's education?

All those worries quickly dissolved once the family arrived.

The compensation package for Edward's new position was even more impressive than she had expected.

The family moved into a five-bedroom, 8,000-square-foot house in Alpharetta Georgia, just outside of Atlanta. Not only was the payment for the house handled through the church, but Edward received a monthly salary of $7,000 tax free, with added bonuses for membership increase.

The newfound wealth gave the family a sense of freedom that they had never experienced before, and Edward had nothing to worry about except preaching God's word. At least that what he thought.

Solid Foundation Cathedral became the focal point of the family's attention. The church was every bit of what Travis had told them and more. Upon entering the 1,300-seat sanctuary, Frank could see why it was so attractive to the average person. In the foyer, you are immediately greeted by soaring ceilings reminiscent of a cathedral. There was a rose window above the central entrance to the church. The segments of stained glass radiated out from its center like unfolding petals of a full-blown rose. The church was a brick structure with a steeple that reached high above the church. There was a lobby with four entrance points to the sanctuary in circular positions. The sanctuary's pews faced towards the pulpit with four long aisles. The pulpit was raised, with an entrance off to the right for the pastor. The windows were stained yellowish with pictures of praying hands and bibles, indicating that you were standing in a holy place of worship.

Frank could barely hold back his excitement as the Deacon with the heavy southern drawl, walked the family through the church.

Deacon Foster led the family toward the pastor's study and encouraged everyone to sit down, as he offered to bring cold sodas to the family. Frank could not believe how large the study was. The pastor's study at Vine Street Pentecostal was a small dingy janitor's closet with a desk, adjacent to the communal bathroom. Visiting ministers preferred to walk straight to the pulpit because nothing was sacred from the thin walls. Whether it was a church mother gently splashing water and humming softly to herself, or the rattling of toilet paper after a burly Deacon had deep-sixed a turd. If only Pastor Ford could have seen what his father had stumbled into.

Edward stood in the corner full of excitement as he scanned the office. Mariyah sat on a small loveseat near the window and thought about how God was blessing them. Edward walked over to Mariyah and sat next to her and gently nudged.

"So, what do you think first lady? Is this something that you think that you can get used too?"

They both smiled at each other and Edward embraced her. He kissed her on the forehead and tried to summarize everything they were thinking.

"Can you imagine this? A couple of months ago, we were in Cincinnati wondering how God was going to bring us through, and now look at us. We are truly blessed!"

Mariyah began to sing her version of "Be Grateful" by Walter Hawkins when her train of thought was interrupted.

Frank was spinning gleefully in the large, cushioned, executive chair until it slammed against the desk.

Mariyah forgot about the song and snapped her fingers in Frank's direction. Her eyes became stern and her teeth squeezed against her month and she whispered and shouted at the same time.

"If you don't get your narrow butt out of that chair, I'm going to kill you."

Frank gave the chair one last spin for amusement and smiled.

Frank was thrilled for the family, especially his father. Edward had often preached about being patient and God would provide, but this was unbelievable. God's grace and favor was pouring down on the family like a thunderstorm.

The feeling of joy quickly dissipated as he sat gazing at the person accompanying Deacon Foster.

"Pastor, you remember the assistant pastor, Vance Williams! He will be working closely with you until you take control of the day-to-day operations."

Vance Williams was a sight to behold. His hair was midnight-black, and it was styled into a short bob. He was lanky with feminine mannerisms, and his Adam's apple made his neck look swollen.

Vance shook hands with Edward and Mariyah and waved at Frank as if he were sprinkling the air with glitter.

"Hi Franklyn!"

Frank quickly looked in his father's direction and then back at Vance, as if something strange had occurred.

Vance stood near Edward and Deacon Foster and whispered.

"Pastor, we really need to get a couple of things taken care of at that bank. You know, with the building and a few other things. It shouldn't take that long."

Vance's voice was high pitched, and he sounded like a man trying to talk like a woman.

Edward's eyes hardened as he glared in Vance's direction. He swallowed and his teeth began to grind together slowly. It was like he wanted to say something, but this was not the place or time.

Watching Vance pussyfoot around his office with all the exaggerated movements of his hips and shoulders, had Edward contemplating if everything in front of him was worth it.

Edward stared at Vance and thought about that passage from Deuteronomy, "God will not bless an abomination."

Before Edward could even find the words to say, I gave him the speech!

"You see Edward, that's your problem. Somebody gave you a gift horse and you're already about to screw it up. So, what if half the people in your congregation are gay. You could be in a worse predicament. You could still be in Cincinnati slaving down on Vine Street in that piss hole. Did you not see that compensation package? These people are paying you $100,000 dollars a year, just to tickle their ears on Sunday. You have everything you ever wanted and here you sit thinking of a way to screw it up."

Edward's first sermon had been anticipated for weeks. People who had not attended the church in months sat in the audience, puzzled and also curious. Who was this no name minister from Cincinnati? And more importantly, why had he been given the reins to one of the largest churches in Atlanta.

Frank had seen his father prepare for a sermon hundreds of times, and it usually was the same method. He would pray and seek wisdom from God regarding the needs of the congregation. Then he would just start writing on sheets of paper. Some sermons come easily in a few hours, while others took days. But it was a process that only God and he knew about. This was the first time that Frank had ever witnessed his father's sermon critiqued.

Edward may have had the auditory skills to make a hummingbird land on his shoulder, but the church's board of directors surely was not going to allow him to be unleashed without certain expectations.

Edward's first sermon was critiqued, scrutinized, and reworked for weeks before being approved. He may have hated the process, but the board of directors were leaving nothing to chance!

On the day of the sermon, Frank knew something was a little off when Vance introduced Edward as Dr. Edward Barkley.

Doctor?

Edward had barely graduated the ninth grade! And suddenly, he had a doctorate degree in divinity.

Don't get me wrong; I certainly understand the concept behind the board's decision. Words coming from a person with a Ph.D., carries a lot more weight than Pastor Edward Barkley, two credits shy of graduating tenth grade. But how could you look yourself in the mirror and be proud, let alone your family.

They know you!

At least, Frank thought he knew his father.

Frank had no idea that the board of directors had sent in a couple hundred dollars to one of those unaccredited theology schools, that hand out degrees to famous preachers for free publicity. In the forty-eight hours that it took to process the payment, Edward graduated high school, college, and graduate school without submitting any work or receiving any grades.

Edward rose from his kingly chair and walked in a dignified manner towards the rostrum.

Surly Mariyah would say something to Edward and stop this charade, but she didn't. She simply stood proudly and applauded like the rest of the board members.

Frank was confused at what he was seeing. What happened to the man who could not be bought or sold? Surely Edward would choose to hold strong to his beliefs and renounce the board's directives, but he didn't. He had too much to lose now.

In Frank's mind, Edward should have said that this is wrong. He should have been irrepressible with his resolve. He should have made it clear that it went against all his beliefs. What does it profit a man to gain the whole world and lose his soul? Wealth is temporary and at death you leave everything behind. All of the honors and bank accounts are nothing without seeking the giver of life first.

But Edward simply stood before the congregation with an arrogant smile on his face.

Frank may not have understood why his father was betraying his faith, but I understood perfectly.

It would have been hard for Edward to look his wife in the face and tell her that he can't accept the money. It would have been hard telling his family that they have to give up that beautiful house in Alpharetta and move back to that ugly shotgun house in Cincinnati.

As I said before, I don't make you do anything against your will. I just give you a hard lesson in reality. And the reality of the situation was that Edward had no intention of going back to what he had come from. His life was finally coming together, and he would be damned if he gave it up for his convictions.

Frank never forgot the look on his father's face as he walked away from everything that he believed to be true. His father had an almost defeated look on his face as he opened his mouth and went from a soldier in Christ's army to a Four-Star General in mine.

"Let us bow our heads!"

"Almighty Father, creator of Heaven and earth and everything in between, we humbly come before you with thanksgiving in our hearts, asking for your never-ending mercy. We lift Your name on high, above any name that has ever existed, our father and creator, we ask you to release your supernatural favor upon us. God, we ask you today for divine intervention in all areas of our lives, be it a new job, promotion, or freedom from debt. Please send double portions anointing and blessings in the quickest time to the people in this building who invite friends and family to the new and improved Solid Foundation Cathedral."

'Let the church say amen, will somebody help me celebrate as God releases his blessings down."

The audience responded with a thunderous "amen!"

"My God is an amazing God, Amen!"

Again, church members responded, "amen!" "all right," "that's right," "come on," "help him Lord," and "preach the word."

"Somebody touch their neighbor and say neighbor, God will make a way out of no way!"

The audience repeated Edward's words verbatim and began to clap and cheer as if they were powering Edward up. Edward's voice became melodic, and he began to sing the words.

"Hallelujah!"

"Hallelujah!"

"Every time I think about the goodness of Jesus, and what he has done for me, my soul cries out!"

"Hallelujah!"

Frank could not believe that his father was doing the exact same thing that he despised about Pastor Ford, at Vine Street Pentecostal.

The congregation's excitement swelled to a fevered pitch, as they clapped and began to shout. The ushers, clad in all white and looking like emergency nurses, rushed to the most out-of-control people overcome by the Spirit. They surrounded them and held hands as if making a human circle and allowed them to bounce back and forth like an out of control pinball crashing into bumpers.

The excitement began to dissipate as Edward continued his message slowly. Edward's deep baritone voice matched the state-of-the-art sound system perfectly, as his voice echoed throughout the large auditorium.

"Saints let me tell you how God blessed my family and me! Before we moved to Atlanta, God tested me to see if I was ready for my blessing. You see, saints, my family and I were struggling financially in Ohio. I would take two steps forward and the devil would knock me back ten steps. On Easter Sunday, I gave the word to God's people. And when I got finished delivering his message, they gave me a love offering for one thousand dollars. I was so happy because I finally had a little money, and I could take care of a couple of things."

Frank looked at his father first, and then at his mother in amazement. She was laughing and shaking her head in agreement. Frank remembered vividly what had occurred on that Easter Sunday, and the story that his father was telling was not true. Frank swallowed hard as his throat slowly began to dry.

Edward glanced in Frank's direction briefly and continued to spin the biggest lie that he had ever envisioned.

"God knows we needed that money! We had no groceries in the house, my son needed a new pair of shoes, and I had twenty dollars left to my name. Saints, we were in the deep end of the ocean without a life jacket, and we were taking in water. Saints, we were going down fast! Do you know what the Spirit told me?"

The audience responded in one voice, "what did it say pastor?" , curious and engulfed in Edward's tale of God's blessings.

 "He told me to give it back!"

The congregation gasped loudly as if shocked about what was being said. Edward's voice tone went up three or four octaves into a primal scream as he repeated what he had had just said.

"That's right, saints, the spirit told me to give the money bAAACK!"

The entire congregation was on the edge of their seats, listening intently as Edward painted the perfect picture of God's grace and mercy.

And I thought to myself, well God, I have $20 to my name, we need food, and you want me to give this money back to the church?

People laughed and nudged each other as Edward paced back and forth on the stage like Chris Rock ready to deliver the punchline.

"I grabbed the envelope, shook it a few times, and gave it back to the Pastor. I raised my hands toward Heaven and started praising God. People around me thought God must really be blessing him to give back that type of money and then praise God afterward.

Edward suddenly stopped and pointed at the audience.

No! That wasn't it!

The audience erupted into laughter as he continued.

"I was absolutely desperate! I was begging God to show me a way out! God! God! Why are you making my family suffer? Why are you putting me through all these trials and tribulations without ceasing? You see, at the time, all I could see was me and my family starving and no place to live. I couldn't see the end of the storm."

The congregation roared to life, and people yelled, "just be patient, God will make a way!"

Edward pointed at the audience.

"That's right saints, he will make a way. So anyway, fast forward to the end of the service. We left the church that Easter Sunday, went to bed hungry, but I was still begging God for a miracle. The next morning, I heard a knock at the door, you know who that was?

The audience begged Edward to reveal who it was as he mockingly smiled and looked around the large church.

"It was Brother Askew's son, Vincent, knocking at my door and he gave me $20,000 and the keys to this church."

The crowd was uncontrollable as Edward strutted around the pulpit. People ran to the pulpit and started throwing money toward Edward like he was the main attraction at Magic City.

Edward took a deep breath and screamed a final quote to the audience.

"He provided all my needs because I had risked it Alllll."

If this had been a grange concert, the audience would have probably destroyed the stage in gratitude. But at Solid Foundation Cathedral, gratitude was shown in the form of money. People ran to the pulpit and chunked thousands of dollars at Edward's feet as he hummed along while the choir sang, "You can't beat God in giving, no matter how hard you try."

Edward had warned Frank that the best deceivers mix truth with lies, pull you in by promising that God will bless you with more money, but first, you must give all to him. Now his father was doing the same thing.

My scheme against a great man like Edward was to break him down brick by brick until he no longer desired for Christ to be in his life. You just don't wake up one day and decide to throw your faith away, It's a gradual progression of compromises that lead to something bigger. You overlook small insignificant sin; start negotiating with me, and then finally turn your back on Christ.

Chasing riches in God's name and calling it a blessing rather than a gift from Satan, was the first time that Frank witnessed his father compromise his faith. But it was only the start.

The more compromises Edward made in his new position, the more offers I made.

What do I care about how special Edward was in Christ's army, he works for me now! When he said yes to the big church, the money, the house, and the car, he was mine.

This was the money game!"

And the money game it was!

Whoever tells you that money won't change them is a lie! Money changes people because it consumes you. Edward fell in love with the power, prestige, and pride attached to money.

Comfortably living out the American Dream in a million-dollar home was a small expense to me; if it meant him turning his back on Christ.

His agenda went from bringing love and unity into the lives of Christians to an agenda filled with lies, deceit, and pursuit of money. And once you agree to my terms, you best believe there's fine print. And my fine print can have you trapped in a 360-degree contract from hell, literally!

Frank saw how the different concessions made by his father, were taken a toll on the family. Frank hated that his father was constantly on the road doing speaking engagements. The family no longer struggled financially, but the family lost Edward.

When I say lost, it doesn't mean he left the family. He just allowed my priorities to become his priorities. And what are my priorities? Destroying as many lives as possible through deception.

You see Christ may have done his little spiritual thing on the cross, but I still control the physical world you live in. I can still wreak havoc on your life by lying, deceiving, and corrupting everything that is good in your life.

Allegations of Edward cheating with Valencia Thomas was the latest concession, but by far the biggest one. Edward denied the allegations, but it was apparent that something had occurred.

Edward had been excessively protected by the church board and elders at Solid Foundation Cathedral. They allowed no one to get close to him, especially the little church groupies sprinkled throughout the congregation. The Church groupies were equal to and in some cases more calculating than their counterparts in entertainment and athletics. The groupies chasing after athletes or entertainers had the Laws of Probability in their favor. The large pool of hard penises assured that there was always at least one lonely soul in the music group or on the football team.

Church groupies had to be more cunning and devious. Pastors at mega-churches like Edward, always had someone watching. The ushers, deacons, elders, and the congregation. It made it hard to get next to Edward. The fanatic searching for the Pastor's admiration had to be twice as sharp.

They first had to be smart enough to convince the Pastor's inner circle that they could be trusted. They usually started by joining any committee that gets them near the Pastor's handlers. They work hard and show that they can be loyal. Eventually, they are promoted to an assistant position around the Pastor's trusted circle. They would hang out at important church events and get acclimated with the Pastor's inner circle. Once they get familiar with the Pastor's inner circle, they started placing themselves strategically in places to introduce themselves personally to the Pastor. Once they initiate contact with him, they had to make him feel comfortable.

The most important level of access for a church groupie is trust. A pastor must be able to trust that woman with the ultimate betrayal, living a lie. The essential goal of a church groupie is to have total access to the Pastor and gain acceptance into his world. The church elders had a lot of experience with church groupies gone wild, so they made sure the inner circle around Edward was tight. That's why it seemed a little odd to Frank that a woman like Valencia could get so close to Edward in such a short period.

Valencia's intent did not appear to be seductive or malicious at first, but her actions had shown that she was extremely treacherous.

Frank had seen the hurt in his mother's eyes whenever Valencia came around. And on one hot July morning, it became apparent that Valencia's status had gone from just a church groupie, to a major disruption in the Barkley household.

Rumors about Valencia's misconduct had begun to circulate shortly after she took a leave of absence from the church. Now there was no doubt about her misconduct because she was holding a newborn baby. In other words, unless she was the Virgin Mary, she had some explaining to do.

Edward glanced down at the podium nervously and slowly arranged the papers in front of him. He understood that the matter with Valencia had to be addressed with a public admonishment, but he also knew that this was a delicate situation. The embarrassment of cheating on his wife was bad enough, but couple that with a public repentance which implicated Edward as the father could turn into a public nightmare.

Edward and his handlers were dealing with the situation delicately. There was no proof that Edward was the father, but the implications were enough. Jamal Bryant's affair ended his marriage, disrupted his congregation, and almost destroyed his ministry. Can you imagine adding a love child to that equation? It would have been Jessie Jackson's discovered love child on steroids.

Valencia's baby resembled Edward, but the paternity test had come back negative long ago. No one really knew why Valencia showed up to church on that particular day, but it was assumed that one of Edward's pastoral enemies had something to do with it. Valencia had always remained silent about their affair even after the paternity results. Best guess was that one of his adversaries wanted to see him squirm while he was on national television.

Edward seemed uneasy as he instructed the deacons to escort Valencia to the front of the church. The Mothers of the church, who normally advised the young women in the church, now had looks of disdain on their faces. In their eyes, she deserved everything coming to her.

Edward searched for words to say as she got closer, but he seemed nervous. Valencia hugged her newborn baby and kissed him. She glared back at Edward, almost daring him to speak.

The uneasy silence in the church was interrupted by Edward's deep baritone voice.

"I know everyone is expecting me to admonish this sister publicly for her sins. You come to these types of services and see me, and you automatically think that it's easy. Well, I'm here to tell you that it's not. Sometimes God leads me to do something else, but I disobey him just to make the church happy. Well, I refuse to do that anymore. God does not want me to conduct a public admonishment with this sister today; he wants it to be private. And for the first time in a long time, I'm going to obey him."

Edward's favorites cheered loudly and applauded, as Valencia walked back to her seat. Most of the congregation sat and stared in astonishment. Valencia glanced around the room in amusement as the congregation's eyes stayed fixated on her newborn baby. They could not believe what they were seeing! Edward simply sat down in his chair and signaled the choir to start singing. Sure, people were whispering about the biased treatment of Valencia, but no one dared question Edward.

It had been years since anyone in Solid Foundation Cathedral had questioned Edward. Besides, questioning him would only lead to one being ostracized. Edward took full advantage of these situations because he knew how powerful he had become.

Frank simply stared blankly at his father, sitting in the pulpit not knowing who he had become. Anyone who had eyesight could see that there was more to this story.

At first, Frank could not understand why his father had slept in the guest bedroom for the past year. He had been told it was because he snored too loud, now he understood.

At first, he couldn't understand why his mother had cried so much and always seemed depressed. He was told that it was because she missed her family back in Cincinnati, now he understood.

As Frank glared at his father with a pompous grin plastered across his face, he finally understood that his family was living a sham. He felt sorry for his mother who was fighting back the tears, but he blamed her also because she had been complicit in the charade.

Frank would have preferred that his family had remained in Cincinnati poor and together, rather than wealthy and destroyed.

For the first time, Frank realized that his family had been destroyed by greed and power. His mother had lied all this time just to save face. Nobody would have cared if a few family members talked about her being poor? At least she would have still had her self-respect. She compromised her faith for the lifestyles of the rich and famous.

It was nothing like showing up for her family reunions and being treated like royalty. No more raggedy cars, no more dusty outfits from the Salvation Army. She now switched cars out like pairs of socks, and all her clothes and jewelry were custom made. People no longer laughed behind her back, just everyone standing and looking in admiration.

I made the feeling especially intoxicating for her so she wouldn't want to go back. I couldn't have her criticizing Edward and making him feel guilty when he was working for me, so I gave her something to shut the fuck up.

Riches!

Edward went from a modest pastor who modeled himself to live a Christ-like life, to a greedy church tyrant. Those practicing spiritual disciplines and being generous with his time to those hurting was out the door. He became a generator of cash for himself, and a double agent working for me.

That little pregnancy scare may have knocked him off course, but he came back with a vengeance and reinvented himself like Peter Popoff.

Dr. Edward Barkley ascended from the ashes as Apostle Edward Barkley. His sermons were no longer the word of God as a divine revelation from the bible, but rather a direct divine revelation from God channeled through his Prophetic intercessions. He now could prophesy, heal, deliver, and pronounce blessings.

He leveraged Solid Foundation Cathedral as a money-making vehicle! The church paid television and radio stations to air his sermons, and his sermons were just infomercials to promote his books and other products. All those times, he stood in front of the church and millions of followers proclaiming that God had spontaneously given him the ability of prophetic intercession, were tainted.

Edward's TV show was the most-watched show for a pastor in that time slot. He would call people up to the altar and paint their forehead with cinnamon and mango smelling consecration oil. Then he would whisper in their ear and proclaim, "it is done! Whatever you asked of God has been given to you."

People would fly backward like someone had just shot them out of a cannon. And then he would scream, "Wham! A double dose of the Spirit!" and again, the person would fall back and convulse in ecstasy while he paraded around slowly and triumphantly like a WWF wrestling champion looking for the audiences to applaud.

I would just laugh at the irony of what Edward had become.

This was the same person who I had personally seen resting in the Spirit several times back in Cincinnati. Now he was hiring actors to mimic Christ's Spirit because the Spirit had long left his presence.

If God's Spirit had come to Edward, it would have probably scared the shit out of him!

He stopped being guided by the Spirit of Christ and built himself into a money-hungry predator, with CEO tendencies.

When sister Harris sent Edward a sad message about suspending her tithes temporarily for financial reasons, Edward was quick to respond with a message.

"I am sorry to hear that you are having difficulty making your mortgage payments; however, you have to place God first. God will always help you find a way even if it's a struggle for you. It's not clear to me if you have other income in addition to your job at the post office, but you will never be able to pay him back by cutting his portion short. God has given me a prophetic vision about you, sister Harris. I see several trees full of leaves surrounding you. And written on one of the trees is "seven-fold blessing." I don't know what it means, but I believe that it's a message from God. God bless you, and I have no doubt that God will help you make the right decision!"

 Let's just say sister Harris found a way to continue tithing, even if it meant getting a second job.

I followed Frank outside that day, and I was amazed at that heartbroken, seventeen-year-old, begging for Christ to make him stronger in his faith.

I would have been less than a man if I hadn't offered him a position with me.

I stuck my hand out and wrapped my arm around his neck and sat beside him like a long-lost brother, who had been betrayed.

"I know what you're going through bro! If that had been me, I don't think I could have let him live.

Frank stared deep into my eyes knowing who I was but afraid to ask. So, I just continued talking to him.

"I mean, how can you even want to live after that type of shit? How can you walk around happy, knowing that all those family events, Christmas memories, and family outings were nothing but a lie?   All those times your father was sitting at the dinner table cracking jokes to your mom, his dick was smelling like Valencia's pussy. If I were you, I would just kill that motherfucker and go play in traffic."

Frank started chanting Jesus, Jesus, Jesus over-and-over again like an out of control mantra.

That motherfucker sounded like Tina Turner, "Nam Myoho Renge Kyo," when Ike was about to put his foot in her ass.

 It must have taken a lot of strength to ignore me, but he did. He just kept calling on Jesus and asking God to forgive those who had hurt him.

The poor boy looked beat up on enough, so I just left him there searching for answers about his faith.   I could have destroyed Frank that day because he was vulnerable, but I didn't.

He just sat there mumbling.

"I'm going to destroy your kingdom one day."

I could have taken his threat seriously, but why? I mean, think about it. Do you know how many people have vowed to destroy me or get retaliation for something that I did to them? Do you have any idea of how many times I've heard a beat down Christian promise to do better after getting out of trouble? I don't have time to sit around scared; my job is to destroy your relationship with Christ, and I do a damn good job of it.

Frank fell off my radar while he finished navigating his way through high school, but I knew he would come for me eventually. It was like he took me destroying his family as personal.

Don't get me wrong, I understand. "Whatever doesn't kill you better start running. I mean, do what you do! Shoot your best shot!" I got all the time in the world.

But Frank was doing the most, and it was really starting to annoy me. I was smiling at his insults, but I was wishing that I had killed that motherfucker when he was on the steps babbling.

Some people can't take that type of pressure, and they turn to whatever self-pity device available to them even if it means death. And then you have people like Frank, who fight back and take refuge in Christ.

Frank gave his life to Christ and moved to Chicago and started taking classes at the Moody Bible Institute. He immersed himself in the word and convinced himself that he had become better, greater, and smarter by facing that adversity.

He stopped asking why Christ allowed me to destroy his family and started formulating a response. He turned his righteous anger into a force for doing good. He redirected his frustration with injustice and unfairness and channeled it into a drive to fight against me. He allowed his outrage for his parents' failures to propel him into direct action against me. When he saw innocent people suffering, he helped them. He took Ephesians 6:12 so seriously that he tattooed it on his back as a reminder of my power. He made that verse part of his daily prayer in high school.

Every morning after his encounter with me, you could hear him muttering.

"We are not fighting against flesh and blood, but against evil spirits and workers of iniquity. Lord give me the power to combat and destroy Satan's works and turn the pain that he causes in the world to Godliness."

Frank was the highest-ranking student in the graduating class. He graduated Summa Cum Laude and he was asked to give the valedictorian.

You should have seen the way he mocked and demeaned me during his speech.

"Parents, faculty, and fellow classmates, I know that valedictorian speeches are often something more to be stoically endured rather than rapturously enjoyed. But I will try to keep your attention and present an experience you will never forget. I can't promise how everyone will react to what I'm about to say, but I only hope that you remember."

"Even if your sins are deeper than the ocean, Christ will forgive you! Given your life to Christ is something you have to do every day. Satan, the enemy of your soul, puts every possible obstacle in the way because he is seeking to subvert your life of faith. You have to use all the means of grace, especially Bible study, prayers, and Christian fellowship, to build yourself up so that you are prepared for spiritual warfare. When you become a Christian, you enter into warfare with Satan. Remember, don't lose your cool, just be still and let God fight your battle. Sometimes the people in your household will turn into your worst enemies, but you have to be strong! You might even find yourself at war with everyone around you, depending on how bad Satan wants your soul, but you have to hang in there. And always remember, once you decide that you want to walk a new path, Satan will never back off. He hates when you make him look bad. The more shame you cause him, the more he will try to wreak havoc in your life."

Frank's parents were seated near the front of the auditorium as Frank delivered one of the most profound speeches, slash sermon, ever witnessed at the Moody Institute. His voice was overwhelmingly powerful, mesmeric, and soothing. The audience was captivated by him. The happy smiles and roar of the audience only made the moment more special when they applauded for several minutes after he was finished.

Frank's mother and father were almost doubled over with the pain of conviction. It was like there was something powerful, revealing that they were shackled, and it was time to correct it.

Conviction from the holy spirit is the one thing that I fear most because the outcome is uncertain. Conviction from the spirit involves choices in moments regarding something you've already done, or are about to do. The choices are simple yet powerful. Get right with God now and be free or continue down the same path and suffer. No matter who you are, it can be a defining moment in a person's life, and I rarely come out the victor under these circumstances. That person may not change that day, but that feeling of conviction never leaves. It's like labor pains twisting and turning inside them until they ask for forgiveness.

All I could do was stand back and hope for the best because God was speaking to Edward and Mariyah personally through Frank. Both Edward and the other caravan of members who traveled from Atlanta to Chicago to see the graduation were in awe of what they were seeing. It takes years of experience before you can speak conviction and upliftment in the same sermon or speech, and here Frank was already doing it with great accuracy.

Edward and Mariyah may have been under conviction, but board members from Solid Foundation Cathedral saw Frank as the future.

A double major in Religion and Marketing made Frank a hot commodity before he even made a name for himself.

Several board members cornered Frank after his graduation with a salaried position to come back to Atlanta and be Solid Foundation Cathedral's youngest assistant pastor while he finished his studies at Morehouse College, but Frank declined.

Frank was still holding resentment toward his father, and he had no intention of receiving his teachings.

Edward understood, he wanted his son to be with him in Atlanta, co-pastoring, but how do you make amends to a person who is not ready. Edward had extended the olive branch several times to Frank, but Frank simply saw it as his father's guilt. The thought of Edward cheating on his mother had destroyed him, and that probably was the single most important reason he accepted Christ into his life in the first place. He didn't accept Christ out of conviction; he did it to show his father that he could be a better man than he was. Frank wanted to show Edward that he didn't have to sell his soul for a few trinkets of gold. And he certainly didn't have to risk the family's reputation by cheating with a church groupie.

Frank chose instead to move to Cincinnati and finish his education at the University of Cincinnati. He also took a lesser, unpaid position as one of the Youth Ministers at St. Stephens Pentecostal Church.

Youth Minister at St. Stephens was the perfect position for him, because it allowed him to grow spiritually without a lot of distractions.

Frank was tired of seeing church leaders more interested in preaching style and entertainment, than in making a difference in the lives of those both in and outside the church. He was tired of seeing church leaders like his father who were only interested in personal prosperity and ignored personal responsibility for those who were lost and hurting. Frank saw his parents' sellout spiritually, but he knew that there was much more to walking in Christ because he had seen it.

Before all the fame and glitz, he saw Christ in his father's life. Frank was willing to sacrifice everything just to find that and he finally found it at St. Stephens Pentecostal Church.

He took his duties as a youth minister seriously. When the other youth ministers shied away from challenges from the senior leaders, Frank stepped up and took charge of the ministry. Frank outworked his peers because he wanted to see his new church grow and thrive. He was the first one to pick up a phone and just say hi or invite a person to come and worship. You could call Frank whatever you wanted: try hard, kiss ass, uppity, but you couldn't deny that he was sincere and a go getter.

By the time his final year at the University of Cincinnati arrived, he had on the whole armor of God.

He was alert and always had his defenses up in anticipation that I would launch a full-blown attack.

I honestly did not start taking him seriously until I saw him in action. I had heard about this guy full of Christ's spirit on the campus, but to me, it was just rumored.

I had seen them all come and go from Moses to Paul; they were nothing to me except flashes in a pan. Sure, they may have saved a couple of souls, but I was still at the top of my game. Not to brag, but whether I'm 2,020 or 4.5 billion years old, I've been whipping the body of Christ's ass. I don't care what type of soldier for Christ you claim you are. You're a joke to me.

So, you could see I wasn't really worried about someone named Frank Barkley. That was until I saw his works.

What does that verse say?

"Wherefore by their fruits, ye shall know them. For a good tree bringeth not forth corrupt fruit; neither doth a corrupt tree bring forth good fruit. For every tree is known by his own fruit."

Love, joy, peace, longsuffering, gentleness, goodness, faith, meekness, and temperance - Frank was nine-fold strong with the fruits that all Christians should be producing in their lives with Christ.

He was aggressive about contrasting everything that I held to be true. He taught and attended bible study regularly, and he was bold about witnessing to others about Christ. He would stand in the middle of the college quad and just babble on about Christ.

"Good afternoon brother, good afternoon sister, my name is Frank. Can I please tell you about what Christ has done for me? Before I accepted Christ into my life, things were ok, but they weren't great. Now I have a lot more to be thankful for. Good things happen in my life every day, and now I'm not afraid to say that God is the one responsible for it. There were things that I was worried about, but Christ has given me a peaceful mind. It's only by the grace of God that I'm here, and I want you to have the same experience. You have to accept Christ Jesus, and his precious holy spirit in your life to combat Satan. Satan will run from you once you start showing the spirit of Christ. Listen to this verse, "Now the works of the flesh are evident, which are: adultery, fornication, uncleanness, lewdness, idolatry, sorcery, hatred, contentions, jealousies, outbursts of wrath, selfish ambitions, dissensions, heresies, envy, murders, drunkenness, revelries, and the likes. Of which I tell you beforehand, just as I also told you in time past, that those who practice such things will not inherit the kingdom of God."

I don't know what it was about Frank; he just had that "it" factor like his father. Pecan brown skin and dark wavy hair, he reminded you of Morris Chestnut. His cheeks were chiseled like a finely-carved statue, and his lips were slightly full, with a seductive smile.

He spoke with confidence, and his passionate testimony could burrow deep into your soul. He was friendly and people could relate to his testimony. And when people laughed at him, he didn't respond with fear, anger, hatred, or ignorance. He responded with compassion, love, and kindness.

He had some of my best soldiers on their knees, begging Christ for forgiveness. It was appalling! Besides, I have a reputation to uphold!

Frank had me standing on the side, looking like Rico from the movie Belly.

"I don't like this shit! I don't like this shit at all. I might have to drop a dime on him."

Every time I turned around, I swear he was praying to God for something!

"Thank you, God, for blessing me. Dear God, please watch over my family. God please send me a holy, righteous, and God-fearing woman."

It got to the point that I had to test him. I wanted to see if he could really hold strong to his faith when he was walking in the middle of a storm. I mean, after all, God only asks that I don't touch you. He never said I couldn't throw a couple of temptations your way to see if you like it. And when it comes to temptations, I have the best! My temptations are like goldmines! My temptations are so good that people start thinking about lies before I even tempt them.

Entry:
Frank's Eve

I must give it to Frank. He was a fighter. His faith kept him in the battle longer than I expected. The special thing about Frank was that he was nothing like his father. It took time and patience, but the lures of money and lust eventually caused Edward to stray from God. This approach wasn't working with Frank. He knew what was coming because he'd seen his father fall, and Frank wasn't having any of it. I hit the kid with gossip, I played on his pride, I assaulted his self-worth and he deflected my attentions like he was swatting flies. I sent seductive women in his path, but unlike his father, Frank didn't stray. Forewarned is forearmed, and he knew better.

This was getting frustrating. I actually had to put some thought into Frank's fall.

I was close to giving up, and then I came up with a brilliant idea. What if I give him what he wants? What if I placed a good, God-fearing woman in his life? Sometimes you need someone in your life that you can share spiritual companionship with! Well, look no further, because I have the perfect woman for you. If God gave Adam his Eve, then I could give Frank his Leeann.

Leeann Carlson was a special girl, a person full of life and energy who could have been the wholesome, spiritual person Frank was hoping for. By the time she met Frank, she sure looked the part. But I knew better because I had been messing with her and her family for years. On the outside, she was everything Frank hoped for in a girl. Attractive, meek, modest, but on the inside, she was mine. Her internal mind, soul, and nature were wild, licentious, and subversive. She was like the perfect red apple with no scratches or blemishes, but her insides were worm-infested and vile.

Yeah! Leeann Carlson was the perfect temptress.

Leeann was the result of an earlier project - the corruption of her God-fearing father, John Carlson, in Dayton, Ohio.

John had plenty of chances to walk away from what I was offering, but he just stopped fighting for God's grace and mercy.

Once I convinced him that he was out of God's grace, he was mine! He stopped going to church, lost sight of what was essential to his faith, and most importantly, became selfish.

John resisted my invitation to leave his family, but he continued cheating. After a year of cheating, I came back and visited with John.

"John, you really are having a great time aren't you. You deserve to be this happy all the time. It can be a screw fest every night, with any woman you want."

That was the night that John decided to leave Leeann and her mother, but more importantly, he walked away from Christ.

Leeann's mother was hurt and embarrassed by the entire incident. She had been faithful to John all those years, and he was running around screwing all these young girls. The hurt turned into hate, and her hate turned into resentment. She decided that John Carlson should be cut off from Leeann's life completely.

What did I care about a wife at home crying about infidelity, or a daughter hurting because her family was destroyed? I found a loyal servant in John, and I rewarded him with three beautiful baby mamas.

I'm sorry, sometimes I fail to mention that everything does not always have a storybook ending on this side.

Ms. Carlson took Leeann and moved into a small apartment in Troutwood, Ohio and vowed to never speak with him again. Leeann and her mother struggled for three years, until Leeann's mother met a man who was good to her. Leeann's mother was not attracted to him, but he was financially stable. I had a conversation with Leeann's mother and suggested that she move in with the man. After all, she deserved more!

John was inconsistent with child support and she needed someone who was more fiscally responsible.

Leeann's mother wanted the best for them, and she was willing to do whatever it took to make their life better.

Julius Stallings was 30 years older than Ms. Carlson, but he offered Leeann and her mother a comfortable home in Vandalia instead of an apartment. He offered them a variety of meals everyday instead of a choice between potted meat and Raman noodles. And most importantly, he offered them financial security. Julius gave Leeann and her mother everything they had ever dreamed of wanting.

Julius truly loved Leeann's mother, but Ms. Carlson was confused about her feelings for him.

Sometimes I had to speak through that confusion just to get what I wanted. And what I wanted was Leeann. I mean, think about it! Why would I want someone old and crusty to do my work? I get more satisfaction playing with souls fresh off God's assembly line.

Every time Ms. Carlson thought about not being in love with Julius and leaving, I showed her that one-bedroom apartment, refrigerator with empty shelves, and empty checking accounts.

I know it was wrong! But I had to keep her focused!

I spoke with Ms. Carlson about how a loveless relationship could still benefit her.

"If you meet a nice man like Julius, you don't walk away from that situation because of a lack of love. You embrace it! It's not every day you get the chance to be financially comfortable and sacrifice such a small part of you. Leeann is happy and just think of all the money you get, especially when he dies. Just make him comfortable for now and find some hobbies to enjoy. If it were me, I would start by finding the best parties in town."

Ms. Carlson agreed to marry Julius, but she also started partying with the younger crowd.

Julius complained at first, but after a while, he just fell into a routine and accepted her behavior.

At first, Ms. Carlson felt guilty about leaving Leeann at home with Julius, so I had a little pep talk with her.

"He's fine with this! Leeann spends her time talking on the phone and watching TV. Plus, he's usually asleep by 7:30 pm. What are you worried about? Besides, you deserve to have a life too."

That was about the time that I started given Julius curious suggestions about Leeann. Julius noticed that Leeann was getting older and her body was starting to develop. He discovered this innocently, but as I've stated before, I have a way of turning curiosity into my opportunity.

I painted a picture of Leeann wanting Julius to watch her nude body and possibly allowing him to go further. I also brought it to his attention that she was probably having the same feelings about him. He remembered how she hugged him when he gave her a cellphone for Christmas. That was certainly more than just a thank-you hug.

Julius was a good guy, and at first, he did a great job of ignoring me. But you have to understand something! I can be cunning and ruthless at the same time. I wanted Leeann's soul, and the only way that that could be achieved is through her pain.

The more Julius fought my suggestions; the more Leeann stayed on his mind. One night, Julius walked to his stepdaughter's room and so I gave him a simple suggestion.

"Tell her that you love her and then rub her on her back."

Julius was nervous and started a conversation about her day at school. She responded with joy like any daughter would when their father or caregiver showed them attention.

She was happy that Julius was in her life. Leeann always felt more comfortable around her stepfather and shared a closer bond with him because they had similar personalities.

All the pain and anger that her mother felt towards her ex-husband turned her into an alcoholic, neglectful, and often verbally abusive mother. At times she had zero patience or encouragement for Leeann.

Julius was the total opposite. He had always been there for her, unlike her mother. On those lonely nights when her nightmares came alive, Julius was the person who calmed her fears. When her mother got drunk and cursed her for looking like her father, it was Julius who encouraged her to keep going.

So, when Leeann heard her stepfather say "I love you," it meant nothing to her when she responded innocently, "I love you too."

Leeann's harmless response was my ticket to the pride and lust of Julius. He rubbed her back and then slid his hand down her back and touched her behind.

Leeann froze with fear and questioned what Julius was doing. I also sensed the apprehension in Julius, so I whispered to him, "Tell her that you have a special kind of love for her that nobody understands, not even her mother."

I said tell her that if her mother understood, she would be at home right now. Leeann was young, shy, and impressionable. All she wanted to do was keep the people around her happy.

Julius started kissing Leeann, first on the cheek and then the lips. Julius continued rubbing on Leeann's arms, and he unbuckled his pants. He removed her t-shirt and tried to force himself on her, just as the front door slammed, signaling that Leeann's mother was home.

Julius quickly ran toward the bedroom door in a panic.

"Remember! Don't tell your mother. This is our little secret."

Leeann's mother came upstairs and saw that Leeann looked like she was having a terror attack.

 And why wouldn't she!

The person she trusted most in her world had just violated that trust. Everything that she thought was perfect in her life had just been turned upset down.

Leeann's mother asked her what was wrong, and Leeann told her mother that Julius had touched her.

Her mother, still intoxicated from partying, called for Julius. Julius pretended not to hear her and never responded. Ms. Carlson found Julius sitting quietly in his bedroom watching TV.

He was sweating profusely, and he looked edgy. She screamed at him and demanded to know what had happened between Leeann and him.

I whispered to Julius' pride and he bristled at her with hostility.

"Who the hell are you screaming at? This is my house! And until you move out or start paying the bills, you will address me as the head of this house."

The response by Julius caught Leeann's mother by surprise because he had never raised his voice to her in the two years that she had known him.

Instead of her pushing the issue, she averted her gaze as if she was the one who'd done something wrong.

Leeann's mother apologized to Julius for overstepping her boundaries but still asked for an explanation as to why Leeann was upset.

Julius looked at Leeann's mother with a sour face, as if he had just gulped down a gallon of unsweetened juice.

"Are you serious? Are you questioning me about what I do in my house? This entire situation is a joke. I tried showing your damn daughter some love and affection, and she accuses me of trying to molest her. I was just trying to be nice to her! And also! Let me explain something to you! Do I question what you do, and what time you come home? When you're out partying until three and four in the morning, where am I? And when you're out screwing around with those young thunder cats, what am I doing? Do you think I'm that stupid? I know exactly what you're doing when you leave this house. Now if you ever get tired of our little arrangement, you're free to leave."

Leeann's mother was still confused about the situation and Julius' response didn't help. Why was he reacting like this if nothing had happened?

Tension was getting high, so I needed Julius to be shrewd and get the situation under control.

He poured Leeann's mother a drink and gazed at her with a sultry stare.

"Nothing happened! I hugged her and helped her change into her nightclothes. She took it the wrong way and I blame myself for that. Maybe it's time you reach out to her father so that she can understand a fatherly relationship more clearly.

Leeann's mother was still unsure about what had happened, but she agreed that Leeann's father needed to be involved more.

"Maybe you're right! Leeann tends to overreact to certain situations. Let me go talk to Leeann and smooth this situation out."

Leeann's mother tried to tell Leeann that she was probably making a big deal out of nothing, but Leeann was adamant about what had occurred. She begged her mother to leave Julius as soon as possible, but that would have compromised my goal.

Again, I whispered to Leeann's mother.

"Why is Leeann trying to break up your marriage? I bet something did happen, but it was probably her fault. Have you seen how tight her shorts have been lately?"

Leeann's mother questioned Leeann about the real reason she wanted her to leave Julius.

"I don't understand, Leeann! Why are you making such a mountain out of a molehill? That man has been good to us. He's given us everything that we ever wanted, and he was there when your father left us. Why do you want to throw all of this away over a misunderstanding?"

Leeann pushed back against her mother's explanation.

"Mom, I know what he did to me, and it's creeping me out. Julius has been nice and kind to me, and I have always looked up to him as a father, but tonight was different. It was like something scary had come over him."

Leeann's mother rubbed her back as if she understood and started to realize that her shortcomings could have possibly led to a misunderstanding.

This incident could have very well put Leeann's life on a positive trajectory if her mother had reacted differently. But you must understand! Misery loves company. I just can't wake up and say tomorrow will be a better day. I can't progress in life, so why would I allow you to progress. My job is to crush any dreams of you becoming successful, and sometimes your kids become collateral damage. A mother's natural reaction, whether human or animal, is to protect their young. It's the opposite with me. I want you to be selfish! I want you to place your fears, wants, and dreams over your child's needs. Why? Because your child's despair, depression, and desolation are more valuable to me than your few trinkets from success.

Leeann's mother chose to sacrifice her daughter for the better things in life. There was no way that she was going to give up her situation, so she compromised with Leeann.

"Leeann, you need to understand that men have certain needs, and sometimes they act stupid to get those needs met. Julius was angry about me partying, so he took it out on you. Instead of him coming to me and telling me what was wrong, he got a little touchy, feely with you. There was no excuse for him doing that, and I promise you that it will never happen again. You like where you live, don't you?"

Leeann shook her head in agreement.

"You like the big house, swimming pool, food in your stomach."

Again, Leeann shook her head in agreement.

"Well, sometimes you have to sacrifice things to keep that."

Leeann was confused about what her mother was asking and simply stared at the floor.

"I will spend more time with you, and I will make sure nothing like this ever happens again.

Ms. Carlson kissed Leeann on the forehead and promised to make sure Julius stayed away from her room.

That's how I help you handle your business!

I help you rationalize your child molesting husband who destroyed your daughter's innocence in one day.

Damn, I'm good!

That's not the first time that's happened, and it certainly would not be the last.

Leeann's mother was more observant of Julius and she began to stay home more, but her drinking increased.

Her relationship with Julius was emotionally turbulent and often abusive. Manipulation, shaming, and humiliation became an everyday part of their relationship. Their relationship was built upon jealousy and possession, rather than love and compassion.

Leeann's mother truly believed that she was nothing without Julius.

Drinking daily became her way of dealing with the relationship. Leeann became collateral damage because her mother was rarely sober. The next time Julius came to Leeann's room, Ms. Carlson was at home. She ignored her daughter's cries for help and allowed Julius to molest her.

Even a proficient master privateer of evil such as myself, still can't believe how susceptible to that demon people are. I would have to say, out of all the demons that I have released on mankind, selfishness can be the most diabolical.

You would think that something deep down inside me would encourage that selfish demon to be respectful of children. But I don't!

I'm comfortable seeing an innocent child's dreams and expectations destroyed.

Are you?

I'm comfortable seeing an innocent child depressed to the point of suicide.

Are you?

And most of all, I'm comfortable watching that child blossom into someone dependent on all my vices, just to bury the pain.

I surprised myself with the way I spoke to Ms. Carlson's fear.

"Do you think it's a wise decision to have Julius arrested? Can you really deal with that type of rejection within his circle of friends? When you and Leeann showed up on his doorsteps, you were flat ass broke. Now look at you! No more dingy clothes and your bellies stay full. Your best bet is to charge it to the game and get your mind right.

Leeann is strong, and she'll survive. And one day, she'll understand that you did all this for her.

The periodic rapes and molestation continued off and on for the next three years until Julius died.

Rumor had it that he had a heart attack while he was molesting Leeann. I can tell you, that was not the truth.

The truth was that he had a heart attack while sleeping, but his death was preventable.

Leeann's mother just sat there motionless as Julius clutched his chest throbbing in pain. It was amazing how Leeann's mother never got around to calling the paramedics.

She just sat beside the bed and watched the man die. She must have had a lot of hatred in her heart, to watch him struggle to breathe for forty-five minutes.

Leeann and her mother looked like the perfect grieving mother and stepdaughter, during the funeral ceremony.

Of course, Julius' biological kids took offense to Leeann and her mother receiving money from the estate, but no one blamed them for his death.

Julius' estate was worth eight million dollars when he died. And after all the family members got their portion, Leeann's mother walked away with two million dollars.

Not a bad trinket at the expense of your daughter - if you do right by me, I will always do right by you.

Leeann's relationship with her mother was contentious most days because she still blamed her mother for allowing Julius to molest her. Leeann's mother was frustrated with Leeann's constant bickering and sexual promiscuity.

Leeann's mother believed that Leeann was just being immature and not focused. Sure, Julian was a sick, perverted, wacko. But she still believed that Leeann was just boy crazy.

Like that time she was caught in the boy's bathroom with four boys. Ms. Carlson was just so angry and embarrassed about the whole situation.

"I can't believe you embarrassed this family like that. You are smart, beautiful, make good grades and you attend one of the best private schools in the city. Why the hell would you just choose to have sex with four boys during lunch? I mean, really? Are you trying to be the neighborhood hoe?

Leeann would just sit quietly in her room, waiting for her mother to pass out from being drunk and steal her car. She started coping with her depressed feelings with drugs and drinking. And when that didn't work, she engaged in casual sex.

Leeann had been using drugs and alcohol since she was fourteen to ease the pain. When Julius came into her room, she visualized him as the cutest boy in school.

The alcohol made her forget about all her problems, and she could be whoever she fantasized.

Instead of her mother helping her, she ignored the problem and shipped her off to her father at age 17. But the transition was hard.

When I started working with Leeann, John was struggling with communicating with her, and that played a major part in my plans. Leeann rarely spoke to John and his girlfriend because she was depressed and dealing with past issues.

One day during an argument between Leeann and John's girlfriend, she left the house and returned the next morning.

When she arrived, she found her father waiting for her with her suitcase. John explained to Leeann that the living situation was not working. He explained to her that the house belonged to his girlfriend, and because of her, he was on the verge of being kicked out. And he suggested that she move back to her mother's house.

Leeann weighed her options and decided that living with her mother, who had allowed her to be molested, was not an option. Leeann decided that moving in with her friend, Tonya, looked far more attractive, but appearances can be deceiving.

Entry:
Spec Ops–Fallen Angels & Spiritual Warfare

Spiritual warfare is real, and I spend every day prowling for girls like Leeann, but sometimes I need assistance. Tonya was engineered perfectly for Leeann's further destruction. On the surface, it looked like she had her life together. She had a condominium in the suburbs, drove a corvette, and had tons of designer clothes. But Tonya was different. Tonya was special to me because she was like one of my demon, special forces soldiers. When I needed to bring down a big game target during Christian warfare, she was my go-to operative. I could depend on her to go deep into enemy territory and come back with the head of one of Christ's four-star generals strapped to her back. But she didn't get like that overnight. Like any great soldier in my army, Tonya had to pass my selection.

I just can't have any old wimp trying to take out generals in the army of Christ. When you join my elite forces unit, you must "put out," and "endure much" suffering. You'll find yourself cold, wet, hungry, tired, and physically beat. Your will to continue will be tested, and sometimes you will even wish for death.

If you make it through all those lonely days and nights, wounded physically and mentally in various ways without quitting, you'll find yourself among an elite group of demons. My elite forces would rather die right now than turn their lives over to Christ.

While Leeann was in Vandalia complaining about the amount of starch in her designer skirts, Tonya was living on the Westside of Dayton, Ohio trying to hold her family together. Imagine a twelve-year-old girl having to watch her seven- and eight- year-old sisters, while worrying if her mother would overdose on crack again. That was Tonya's reality.

Before her grandmother got custody of her, she saw it all. She hated walking outside her apartment complex and seeing her mother flagging down cars; or coming home after a long day at school and finding nothing to eat.

Her grandmother was the only person who had stepped up when her mother went to jail.

Tonya was placed with her grandmother in Desoto Bass Courts, and her sisters were placed in Texas with their father.

In Texas, her sisters thrived with their father's family. Her situation was different. Although she was never mistreated or neglected by her grandmother, she could only afford to do so much for her. And Desoto Bass Courts was still the west side of Dayton.

Cute, with no guidance and supervision, it was only a matter of time before the Bass took her.

The jack-boys in the Bass would hire her to bring naïve men with deep pockets back to the neighborhood.

Even as a 16-year-old, Tonya could con the victim into thinking that she really cared for their safety, or that she had their best interests in mind. Her hair was midnight-black, and it was styled into a short cute bob. She had smooth olive skin with petite- shapely features and her smile made her look innocent. Her natural beauty made you want to stare, and her personality went along with her beauty. She reminded you of Nia Long, in the movie The Best Man. Just short and sassy! With a smile that lit up the room. The tricks never had a chance when they came into contact with her.

She had several ways of hustling the johns into a robbery, but her favorite was the three-date rule. Date number one, she was the cute side piece on the baller's arm. She didn't say much but she took notes and acted impressed with everything he was showing her, especially the lavish jewelry and luxury cars.

Date number two was her opportunity to make the mark feel comfortable. She would invite him to lunch and talk about how busy her life was holding down a job and supporting her grandmother. She spent half the time being a cheerleader to the mark and encouraging him to chase after his goals. She would spend the other half of the date describing how honest she was and convincing him that there was no other person in the world whom he would want to share his life with.

By the time the mark left lunch, he was certain that he had found the woman of his dreams.

The third date was the coup de grace. The third date always involved some type of drama that made the mark want to save her. The mark would get an out of the blue call asking for his assistance because she was stranded and afraid. When the mark found out that she was stranded in the Bass, he would either become captain save a hoe or hang the phone up because he knew he was about to be set up. The captain save a hoes' were the ones found walking down Danner Avenue butt ass naked, after being robbed of everything.

The problem with that hustle was that Dayton was small. And eventually she ended up doing a stint in Department of Youth Services.

The prostitution game became her go-to hustle after she was released from DYS. Tonya could still charm the pants off anyone, but her concentration became centered on the twenty-dollar johns. She understood the psyche of a $20 trick, how he wanted it, where he wanted it, and under what circumstances. Fresh-faced and petite, she had the perfect features like a model without all the garb and make-up.

Being a prostitute in the Bass was like walking in an area filled with landmines. She was either dodging lunatics or the police, but she showed great determination.

I saw Tonya progress from a streetwalking prostitute, to a high-priced escort, to her current position as a madam. During each one of those stages in her life, I took a little something from her mentally and physically, but she remained resolute in her commitment to me.

All those cold nights working the corner in Desoto Bass.

Commitment!

Being choked unconscious by a Gorilla pimp.

Loyalty!

All those lonely nights at the hospital after contracting gonorrhea or going to jail.

Allegiance!

No matter what obstacle was thrown her way, she still pledged her life to me.

Sure, I supplied her with different vices to deal with the emotional impact, but she kept her eyes on the prize.

Tonya opened her mind to a brand new perspective, and I rewarded her with wealth and prosperity.

See, that's the difference between being in my army and being in the army of Christ. I can give you everything you want right now. You don't have to die to get your mansion and streets paved in gold.

I have it here for you now.

The wisdom that I gave Tonya was invaluable and it helped make a difference in her life financially. The world is plentiful with resources, and I taught her how to make the best of those opportunities.

But being successful and making good money was always temporary for Tonya. Had I given her everything, she would have been satisfied. I couldn't afford to have one of my best soldiers content and happy, so I had to make her money fluctuate to keep her focused.

Tonya gave off the facade of wealth and luxury, but in reality, she was spending most of her income on designer goods to promote her image. She may have carried Gucci bags, but her wealth was starting to dwindle.

You have to understand my end game before you devote your life to me because everything is short-lived.   I may allow you to be successful and make lots of money for a period, but that does not mean that you are promised a successful future.

I saw that Leeann was vulnerable, so I gave her Tonya to confide in. I needed Leeann to trust Tonya, because Tonya could confuse her even more and mold her into what I wanted.

Tonya was everything that Leeann wanted in a friend. She listened to her problems without any strings attached, and always gave her great advice. And Leeann was everything that Tonya needed in her life at that moment, young, fresh face, to make her money.

Leeann saw all the money and flash but never bothered to look behind the scenes.

Tonya knew all about Leeann's issues with Julius, but she also understood money. And she also knew it was time that Leeann grew up. Tonya told Leeann that her stepfather may have turned her out, but it was time that she used that knowledge to better herself. Tonya explained to Leeann that she needed to learn to turn off her emotions and turn the situation into just a physical act and get paid. I sensed that Leeann was unsure about entering this life, so I told Tonya to calm her fears with a lie.

"Girl, it's not like you're a crack head prostitute working on the corner, you are beautiful. And some men will pay top dollar just to sit and talk to you. You don't even have to have sex with them. Now you can't beat that!   This is easy money, and the most important thing is you're not on the street or back at your mother's house."

Leeann struggled with the decision to get involved, but I have a way of making what you perceive to be wrong, right. Leeann compromised with Tonya and decided that she would just be an escort, but no sex.

I didn't argue with Leeann, because I knew she would eventually come around. As I said before, "I could care less about what she believed is right, or what she thinks is moral or not moral." If you play on my team, you play full time. Her dreams and thoughts become my dreams and thoughts. What she thought was honest and decent today, will not be what she thinks is moral tomorrow.

I've been around a long time, and I've heard people have the same conversation repeatedly.   All that strong talk erodes away slowly when you find yourself at that impasse of hard choices or hard times. And I'm like Lay's Potato Chips, "I bet you can't just do it once. And I could care less about your vows, guarantees, and promises of not doing it anymore. You exist in my world, I make your decisions for you, and you play fulltime."

At first, she was satisfied with just accompanying lonely men to plays and dinners, but in the end, she was willing to do anything for the money.

Her client, Alvin Jenkins, was a 54-year-old divorced father of five. Alvin was tall with salt and pepper gray hair, but he carried himself like a distinguished gentleman. He didn't smoke or drink, and he never asked Leeann to do anything that she felt uncomfortable doing.

Leeann often teased Alvin that if she had met him when he was younger, she would have married him. Alvin always laughed it off as a joke, but tonight I wanted Alvin to test Leeann.

When Leeann arrived at Alvin's house, she was mesmerized at the sight of the house. It was a six-bedroom, four-bath mansion, with a movie theatre room and a swimming pool.

Alvin asked Leeann to sit down and offered her a drink. He also encouraged her to relax because she appeared to be tense. Alvin and Leeann talked for hours about everything, and Leeann felt extremely comfortable around Alvin. She asked if it was ok if she take her shoes off, and Alvin smiled at her and responded.

"I can do you one better, why don't you stay here tonight. I got plenty of room, and we can just kick back and have fun tonight. We can get some sleep, and I'll take you home first thing in the morning."

Leeann had never been in this type of situation before. She had heard Tonya talk about how clients sometimes develop a good rapport and try to get freebies. But she was unsure if this was one of those situations, and she felt uncomfortable. Leeann quickly excused herself to the restroom and called Tonya.

She called Tonya and explained her situation and asked if she could come to pick her up. Tonya explained to Leeann that coming to pick her up would be impossible because she was on an overnight date herself. Tonya encouraged Leeann to take control of the situation and make Alvin understand that spending the night for sex or just conversation would cost extra.

Tonya ended the conversation by telling Leeann that Alvin was an older man and that he probably just wanted conversation. Tonya encouraged Leeann to relax, and Leeann felt more comfortable about the situation.

When she returned from the bathroom, Alvin directed her to a bedroom adjacent to the master bedroom.

I whispered in Leeann's ear, "You control this situation, not him."

 Leeann abruptly stopped at the door and started walking towards Alvin's master bedroom.

"Look Alvin, I know your one of my best customers, but realize that if I stay tonight, I want double my regular pay. And I don't sleep in the servant's quarters. I sleep in the master bedroom."

Alvin was surprised by Leeann's sudden change in demeanor.

Alvin was under the impression that Leeann genuinely liked him and wanted to spend time with him. He was caught off guard when Leeann brought up business and tried to charge him double.

I quickly assessed the situation and decided that this was a good time to apply pressure. I wanted Leeann on my team for the long haul, and Alvin was the perfect vehicle to accomplish that goal

I whispered in Alvin's ear, "So she has the nerve to come to your house and make demands. Come on Alvin! Don't go getting all mushy and soft. I know you thought she liked you, but you can't turn a hoe into a housewife. Forget about trying to fall in love with this tramp; treat her like the prostitute that she is."

Alvin's tone and manner towards Leeann changed. His eyes narrowed and his voice became more calculating.

"Oh! My bad sweetheart, I thought we were off the clock for the night. But since you're offering, we might as well make the best of a long night."

Alvin opened the door to the master bedroom and directed Leeann towards the bathroom.

As Leeann walked into the bathroom, I told her to insult his manhood and she obeyed.

"I hope you can get your little man up because I would hate to have to please myself for the rest of the night."

I looked at the silly grin on Leeann's face and whispered to Alvin.

"Man, I would beat her down and throw her ass out! Or why not do something to wipe that smile off her face."

Alvin was about to put Leeann out when he decided that he would much rather humiliate her.

Alvin used to treat girls like crap when he was on the streets, but he changed his life. He still had friends connected to the streets, but he tried to stay away from that life. But after listening to Leeann, he felt like reaching back to the streets one last time just to embarrass a loudmouth.

Alvin needed time to get everything set up, so he stalled for time. I suggested that he call his friends, Terrance and Jimmy. They were always down for a good party and they understood the type of pressure I needed in this situation. Alvin was ok with Terrance, but he was uncertain about Jimmy.

Jimmy had all the intangibles for being a loyal servant. The first time I met Jimmy, he was 18 years old at the Ohio State Prison. Jimmy was young, had excellent leadership qualities, and had the balls to curse God.

I offered Jimmy a new life through suicide and he was like, "Screw you! Only a weak person would take his life. Screw the Judge, my family, and Christ. I can do fifteen years standing on my head. I don't even care if you take my soul because I'm already dead."

If Tonya was a special forces demon, then Jimmy was a Four-Star General Demon, because of all the repugnance in his heart. God permits evil as a necessary condition of freedom for all the normal human beings that he has created. But if your free will is to mean anything to you, God must allow demons like Jimmy to exist in the world.

The things that Jimmy had been involved in made even my most skilled demons cringe with detestation. He could kill an entire family, eat a thanksgiving meal, sleep peacefully for eight hours, and do the exact same thing for the next 364 days that year.

The hatred in his heart was infinite. He didn't care about right or wrong, justice or truth, his pleasure derived from the suffering of others. And he would gladly expand his predatory violence beyond death if he could! His hatred was like a bucket with a hole in its bottom that could not be filled.

And I loved it!

When Leeann finally came out of the bathroom, Alvin pretended to come up with a bright idea.

"Since I'm paying for the entire night, I want to fool around for as long as possible, so let me take a little something for stamina."

Leeann laughed out loud and called Tonya.

"Girl, you were right! He's sitting downstairs right now waiting for his stuff to get hard."

Leeann was still talking on the phone when Jimmy and Terrance arrived. Jimmy gave Alvin several Rohypnol capsules and told him to go handle his business. Alvin slowly opened the capsules and dropped the powdery substance in a mixed drink.   Alvin instructed Jimmy and Terrance to wait in the media room until he gave the signal.

Alvin went back to his bedroom and knocked on the door. He overheard Leeann say to Tonya, "Ok girl, I got to go, Mr. Softy is knocking on the door."

Alvin was embarrassed and furious. He had never seen this side of Leeann. He always thought of Leeann as a cute, nice, quiet girl, whom he had considered to be a good friend.

Now he was seeing her for who she really was. A self-centered, egotistical person who was humiliating him. He was embarrassed about what she was saying about him, but I convinced him to remain calm.

Alvin gave her the mixed drink and she guzzled it down asking for more. Alvin obliged her and brought her another drink. She started to ask for another drink, until Alvin told her that she had had enough.

She continued to argue with him about getting another drink until a strong urge to sleep suddenly hit her. Alvin knew the roofies where taking effect, so he gave the signal for Terrance and Jimmy to come to the bedroom.

Leeann was about to dose off when she was startled by a voice saying, "You ready."

Leeann was dizzy and disoriented. She tried to reach her phone, but she was violently pushed back on the bed.

Alvin asked if she was looking for this and handed her a wad of money. Leeann tried to get to her purse, but it felt like someone was on top of her. Leeann tried to fight but she lost consciousness.

 Leeann was in and out of consciousness for what seemed like an eternity. Once when she was losing consciousness, she thought she heard Alvin talking to someone, but was not sure because everything was so blurred.

Leeann was finally awakened by the faint sound of her cell phone ringing. Not only was her head hurting, but her entire body was aching in pain, and she smelled like urine. When she finally was able to focus, she looked at her phone and saw four missed calls from Tonya.

She returned the call immediately and Tonya started screaming.

"Where the hell are you at? I've been calling you all morning."

Leeann was still somewhat tired but managed a weak reply.

"I'm still at Alvin's place."

She squinted at the digital clock and saw that it read 3:45 pm. She searched the room shiftily and then opened the curtain. The sunlight flooded her vision causing her to block it with her hands.

"Do you mean to tell me that I've been out of it for over ten hours?"

Tonya responded, "Yes! What's wrong with you?"

Leeann told Tonya to hold on and searched her purse for the money given to her by Alvin. She found it in the side compartment. Leeann pulled the phone close to her mouth.

"Tonya, I feel funny, and I can't remember what happened last night."

Tonya asked if she had been drinking and Leeann replied yes, but that she could only remember having a couple of mixed drinks.

Tonya asked Leeann if she thought she was drugged, and she replied, "I don't know, maybe!"

Tonya offered to come pick Leeann up, and she agreed.

Leeann turned on the shower and gazed in the mirror. Her face was bruised, and she had cigarette burn marks on her body. Her normally vibrant hair lay limp on her head like a muddled wave cap.

She showered as quickly as possible, but she could feel herself losing consciousness again. Leeann put her clothes on and staggered down the stairs, just in time to hear the doorbell ring.

Alvin blocked the doorway and suspiciously looked at Tonya through the window.

"What do you want?"

Tonya replied, "My friend is in there! Open the door motherfucker! Leeann are you ok?"

Leeann stumbled down the stairs towards the door, and Alvin glared at her.

"Trick, don't ever tell nobody where I live."

Leeann rolled her eyes at Alvin and opened the door to leave. Tonya pushed by Leeann and confronted Alvin angrily.

"What the fuck did you put in my girl's drink? Sick motherfucker out here drugging and raping people."

Alvin laughed at Tonya.

"Bitch, please! She got paid $1500 to be with me for the night, plus I got her on video saying so."

Tonya quickly turned and asked Leeann if that was true, and she tentatively shrugged her shoulders.

Terrance strutted through the doorway of the theater room and smiled and winked at Leeann. He placed his hands around his mouth like a megaphone and hollered for Jimmy. He sounded like a game show host introducing the greatest contestant ever.

"Hey J, come say goodbye to your girlfriend, she's about to leave."

Jimmy came out of the theater room in a wifebeater t-shirt. His pace was swift, but every movement was controlled and calculating. The best way to describe the smirk on his face was that it broadcast depravity. If you've ever had the misfortune of meeting Jimmy, it was usually the last thing you saw before an act of unscrupulous terror visited your life. It's a nagging feeling that you can't shake, like being lost in a dark forest. That disquieting feeling that comes when there's just something not right. That awkward feeling when your instincts are screaming; this person wants to see me hurt and broken.

His smile broadened when he saw Tonya, and his upper lip curled into a contemptuous snarl. His gold tooth gleamed, and his eyes were cold and frightening.

"What's up toy, toy! It's been a long time."

Tonya stared at him silently, totally intimidated as if amazed by the restraint of his true power. Tonya's eyes showed fear, and she stiffened with terror when he pulled her close for a hug.

Tonya remembered Jimmy from her days on the streets in Desoto Bass. He was short with bowed legs. His hair had thinned slightly, and he was no longer a youngster. But his muscles, his body in general, was still very fit. Gunfights from wars gone by had left a vertical puffy scar down the front of his chest. It looked like a zipper implanted in his skin. And that eye! His right eye was cloudy mottled gray, from a fractured eye socket he received while in prison. The kids in Desoto Bass nicknamed him the terminator because he was like a one-eyed cyborg wreaking havoc on their neighborhood.

She not only remembered him vividly, but she had witnessed his uncivilized brutality.

The cruel man who didn't think twice about murdering her mother's best friend over $30 worth of crack.

China would have gladly paid back that measly amount of money if he had given her a chance, but he didn't. He simply locked his massive arms around her neck and strangled her. She scratched and clawed at his arms searching for breath, but he just tightened his grip like a python snake in a feeding frenzy. Her eyes began to swell shut as her body shook violently from being trapped inside a human hangman's gallow.

Tonya recalled how the body relaxed and then crashed to the cold concrete.

She remembered how the residents in Desoto Bass walked away from the public execution, confused about what to do. Snitching to the cops was a no, no in the Bass. And dealing with an animal like Jimmy, your life was certainly on the line.

Tonya stared at his arms in disbelief because he still wore the scars from that frightful evening.

He turned his cold glare from Tonya toward Leeann and spoke as if he was friendly to an innocent child.

What's up baby! We were just watching you. You are amazing!"

Leeann ran in the theater room just in time to see a video image of her on the screen. She was barely conscious, and Terrance and Alvin were taking turns having sex with her.

She could hear someone in the background hollowing with joy.

"Man, that bitch taking all that dick! Fuck that shit, move, it's my turn."

The screen went black as Alvin pushed the remote, turning off the projector.

Leeann turned to see Terrance, Jimmy and Alvin give each other high fives and laughing.

Embarrassed, Leeann quickly ran out of the house and waited by the front door, plotting her next move.

Tonya followed her and asked if she was ok. Leeann was angry because she felt like she got played.

Me being me started talking to her pride and wrath. Leeann remembered how Tonya had talked a trick into giving her extra money after she threatened that he had raped her. This situation was even better because Alvin looked like he had a lot more to lose.

 Leeann kicked the door, ran back in the house, and started yelling.

"I bet when I call the police, you motherfuckers won't be laughing."

Tonya followed Leeann back into the house, shocked at what she was saying.

"Leeann, what are doing? The police! Are you crazy!

The laughter in the house suddenly turned into an uneasy silence as Leeann continued.

"What now bitch? I don't hear motherfuckers laughing now! That's right assholes, how much is your freedom really worth to you? $50, 000? $100,000? $200,000?

You need to stop staring at me stupid and ante-up on some money before I call the police."

Tonya looked at the expressions on the three men's faces and saw the panic on all except one. Jimmy!

Jimmy starred through Tonya and Leeann as if they were not standing there at all. Tonya could tell by Jimmy's reaction, that Leeann had made a serious error in judgment. Have you ever heard that saying, "I could see the Devil in him"? Well, that was Jimmy. He was cunning and nice but could be very sadistic.

Jimmy smiled at Leeann and Tonya and asked if he could handle this situation discreetly outside. Jimmy tapped Terrance and Alvin on the back and told them to relax, and that he would handle the situation. Jimmy walked outside and continued to smile as the door closed, and Leeann and Tonya followed closely behind.

Tonya continued walking and grabbed Leeann by the arm.

Come on Leeann, let's go!

Leeann pulled her arm away and moved toward Jimmy, clapping her hands, pointing in his face, and twisting her neck as if possessed.

"No! We don't need to go anywhere. This motherfucker thinks he can just fall through and get some free pussy. Nah! You must have thought you had a fool on your hands. Bitch, you better get my money!"

Tonya was still trying to go to her car while pulling Leeann.

"Leeann, let's go! You don't know what you're getting yourself into."

Tonya's face was stricken with fear and her voice shivered as she spoke to jimmy, almost pleading.

Jimmy please! She's just angry, but she don't mean anything by it. She just had a little too much to drink, but she straight now! I promise you that we'll leave and everything we'll be forgotten.

Leeann continued to argue but Tonya understood the gravity of the situation. They were way out in secluded Kettering, OH. with the notorious Jimmy Hooks. And to top it all off, Leeann was threatening to call the police on him. Of all the dumb shit she had ever done, this had to be the worst.

If she could just get Leeann's crazy ass to the car and explain what was going on, if Leeann could just shut the fuck up for five minutes so she could warn her about the person drilling holes in them with a cold demonic stare. It was like he was studying them to find the computation of how many of their parts could fit in a garbage bag.

Fearing this moment, Tonya sent one last pleading glance towards Jimmy.

"Jimmy please don't!"

And without saying a word, it was like he snapped his finger like Thanos fitted with the infinity stones.

Jimmy moved forward, blocked the path to Tonya's car, and retrieved a 40-caliber handgun from his rear waistband. Both girls froze as he slowly extended his arm, thumbed the hammer back, and fired. The gun jumped to life with a loud boom. The sound of the gun was deafening, and both girls fell face down in a terrified heap. The bullet grazed Tonya's face and buried itself in a tree.

People who die are said to relive their lives in a flash, just before they take their last breath.

I can promise that Leeann and Tonya had the same experience as Jimmy strolled over to them while they begged and pleaded for their lives.

His voice was intimidating but tranquil as he crouched over them. It was the type of voice that implies that your life is in his hands and that there is absolutely nothing you can do about it.

"I'm not a violent man, but please don't ever think that I give two shits about you two bitches living or dying. I will kill you two hoes, bury you in the backyard, and make it my mission to kill every god-damn person in your family, including your pets."

Jimmy pointed the gun at Leeann and ordered her to sit behind the steering wheel. Leeann quickly opened the door and sat in the car. She tried to compose herself, but her hands were trembling with fear.

Jimmy paused for a split second to make sure he had Leeann's full attention, and then smashed the butt of the gun into Tonya's face. The force of his action knocked out several of her teeth and sent her head flying backward with a loud thump against the car bumper.

Waves of fear engulfed Leeann as she griped the steering wheel tightly and screamed in horror at the top of her lungs. The blood-curdling scream made Alvin and Terrance rush from inside the house towards Jimmy. Tonya was face-down on the ground, and they could hear blood gurgling in her throat.

Terrance held out his arm as if to stop Jimmy.

"Hey Jimmy! Come on man, she looks pretty bad."

Leeann screamed through the closed car window at Alvin.

"Help her Alvin, please! He's going to kill her."

Jimmy glanced at Terrance and Alvin with a menacing smile, and they both quickly backed up. Tonya struggled to find the bumper of the car, and then she slowly pulled herself up to her knees. Jimmy flashed a terrorizing sneer that chilled Leeann's bones. He waited until Tonya was almost to her feet and then slammed the pistol into her jaw again. The gun barrel bounced off her face with a loud roaring thud as it discharged.

Terrance and Alvin were immobilized with fear, not knowing what to do next. Leeann's heart pounded against her chest as she peeped through her fingers at Jimmy.

Jimmy held his gun up and looked at it as if it had malfunctioned. His voice was nonchalant, but his lips were curved into a slight smile.

"Damn! I got to watch that hair-thin trigger; I might fuck around and kill somebody today."

Tonya lay motionless on the ground for what seemed like an eternity, and then finally moved.

Jimmy motioned with his pistol for Terrance and Alvin to come to him. They slowly approached and then were relieved when they saw that she had not been shot. Leeann was crying hysterically, and Jimmy instructed them to put Tonya in the car. They gently sat her in the passenger's seat and slammed the car door shut. Jimmy walked to the driver's side and tapped on the window with his gun.

Leeann sobbed uncontrollably and cried out, "Please don't kill me! I promise I will never say anything about this. Please! Just let us go!"

Jimmy motioned for Leeann to let the window down. Leeann was apprehensive about opening the door when she heard the doors unlocking. Jimmy quickly opened the door and dangled the car keys in her face.

Again, Leeann began to beg and plead for her life.

"Please! I promise you I won't say anything! Please don't kill us."

Without saying a word, Jimmy grabbed her purse and fumbled through it until he found her driver's license. He studied the license and tossed it, along with the keys towards her lap.

He propped one foot on the door frame and held the door open with his hand. He spoke sharply, with a cautionary note in his voice.

"Let me tell you two bitches something. This ain't Disney World, so don't play with me. And this sure as hell ain't the Bank of America. My partner paid you nasty sluts $1500, so his obligation to you is over. If you ever say anything about what happened today, I will kill you! I will come to your fucking address and shove an ice pick in your fucking face! Do you bitches understand me?"

Tears rushed down Leeann's face as she fought hard to catch her breath and agree with him at the same time.

Jimmy tossed an ounce of cocaine towards Tonya, and she responded by weakly nudging Leeann. She was struggling to stay conscious and her voice was breathless and weak.

"Come on Leeann! Just start the car and let's go."

Her arms appeared limp and her head nodded as if she was unstable. Leeann touched her face softly and cranked the car to start.

Jimmy glared at Leeann as if deciding on whether he should allow her to live and finally stepped back from the car and smiled.

"Make sure you ladies have a safe trip home; there are a lot of crazy people running around out here."

Leeann quickly pushed the gear into drive and drove away.

The long ride back to Tonya's condo was made longer because of the awkward silence. Leeann could barely drive because her hands were trembling, and Tonya, in and out of consciousness, quietly stared out the window. Leeann glanced over at Tonya looking for the words to say. She wanted to apologize for getting her involved, but she was lost for words. The sheer terror of what she had experienced was just too terrifying to discuss.

Tonya had always warned her about certain pitfalls, and Leeann's biggest drawback was her mouth.

Nah, I'm lying, it was me! I knew how Leeann could be when I pumped her full of liquid courage, and I loved the way her mouth roared to life when she was high. That shit from Jimmy was just a bonus.

Jimmy and Tonya were soldiers who would do anything to ensure that my kingdom moves forward. As a soldier in Christ's army, you are in search of lost souls. Your job is to capture as many souls as possible and bring them to Christ. And, like any good soldier, you will do anything to satisfy your master. My soldiers are no different, they just operate from a depraved point of view.

You call yours the breastplate of righteousness, I call mine the breastplate of depravity.

You lose your moral aptitude and change into a person that only understands duplicity. Honesty is no longer in your vocabulary! The only thing that sparks your interest is debauchery and deceit. And loyalty! You can forget about that. Your only loyalty is to me.

So, when a person like Jimmy or Tonya straps on a breastplate of depravity, it's no telling who will get injured. Tonya is a great soldier in my army, but on that day, she became a casualty in a chess game for Leeann's soul.

Tonya served her purpose by bringing me information on Leeann to allow me to get closer. Now she was expendable!

Leeann took Tonya to the hospital and they lied about her injuries. They gave some story about Tonya getting drunk and falling down a flight of stairs. The story worked, but their relationship changed. Leeann felt bad about the incident because she didn't follow the rules. Never accept a drink if you didn't see it made, and never threaten to get the police involved no matter what. She broke every rule that Tonya had taught her, and it almost got them killed.

Tonya was never the same after that incident. Tonya blamed Leeann for getting her caught up in that situation because she was stupid. Tonya started receiving less work because it affected her mentally. She started using anything that helped take away her terrifying experience with Jimmy, and it ultimately led to her demise.

Broke, and with no way to support herself, Leeann moved back home with her mother.

Checkmate!

Her relationship with her mother was still strained. She still blamed her mother for not protecting her from Julius, and she compensated by being more promiscuous.

Having sex with men she barely knew gave her a sense of power she never had before.

Her mother stopped drinking, cleaned up her act, and now attended church. She tried to convince Leeann to do the same, but Leeann felt like her mother was hiding behind religion to cover up her past sins.

Her mother appeared to be sincere about her new walk with Christ, but her approach was all wrong for Leeann. Her mother never wanted to address the molestation or murder of her husband, but she always suggested that Leeann turn to Christ.

Leeann saw her mother as a hypocrite. You know the type of people! They get a little Christ in their life and, all of a sudden, they're elevated to a righteous pedestal.

Every time the past issues came up, Leeann's mother refused to discuss them. She would simply change the subject or tell Leeann, "When Jesus died on the cross, my sins were transferred to him, and he paid the price for my forgiveness. You should do the same and you will be free also."

It was like she had stolen money from a company that didn't exist anymore. She didn't get caught at the time, so why should she carry that burden of guilt.

But Leeann wasn't free!

Leeann's mother failed to realize the long-term effects of that type of trauma.

Leeann was hurt, lonely, and depressed, and she was searching for a way to offset those feelings. On one hand, she was searching for love and attention by sleeping with different men because she believed that they could add meaning to her life. On the other hand, she enjoyed embarrassing her mother with her lifestyle. She got a kick at the reactions of the church members when her mother invited them over.

Her mother hated the skimpy clothes she wore when the pastors or deacons came to the house. Their eyes were wide with curiosity, glued to her every movement and admiring the tight fit of her cutoff daisy-duke-shorts. The way she made sure that they were looking and then bend over allowing her skirt to slowly rise, revealing her G-string panties immersed in her perfectly round ass. Or the way their crotches swelled when she unwrapped a lollipop, locked eyes with them, and sucked on it seductively.

Most of them were able to head off Leeann's promiscuous temptations, but every now and then, you would see one of the assistant pastors or deacons parked around the corner waiting for Leeann's mother to leave.

"Good morning sister Leeann, I was hoping I would catch sister Carlson before she went to church. Is she here?"

Yeah, she knew the game!

She knew exactly why they had waited until her mother had left for church and mysteriously appeared at the door.

They wanted to use her to fulfill some other fetish that God forbade them to do to their wives.

For her, it was like therapy!

The abuse by Julius had convinced her that she had to be sexually desirable to have any self-worth. Sex became an escape on several levels. It was like all of her happy chemicals were firing into her neurotransmitters at the same time, producing a euphoric rush and immediate high. She didn't have to be emotionally attached. She had the satisfaction of being found attractive, wanted, and worthwhile, while still escaping any controlling relationship or the possibility of abandonment. If a man even thought about having an emotional connection with her, she dropped him. It was like she was searching for someone to fill a void that would never be filled.

Borderline Personality Disorder was what the doctor said Leeann was diagnosed with. Her mother was disgusted by her daughter's reputation and spent several thousand dollars for her treatment. The endless line of men continued, but Leeann eventually pulled her life together enough to attend college.

I guess you're probably saying, "Ok Satan, you've done enough to this poor girl's life. Let her breathe!"

But I needed her for one more task!

Entry:
Frank's Temptation

The moment she left Dayton to attend college in Cincinnati, I knew she was right for this mission. Her mother believed that Leeann would change if she were in a new city, with new surroundings. And for the first semester, she was a new person. She never searched for attention, nor did she seek popularity. She avoided the popular campus venues and parties, preferring the solitude of the library. Intellectual conversations and being successful appeared to be the only thing that sparked her interest. She went from being the neighborhood whore in Dayton to the cute, quiet, first-year student sitting in the corner.

Frank would never have surrendered his faith to my typical girls gone wild, video-vixens, with fake boobs and butts like his father. He wanted an intellectual, quiet, modest girl.

Frank hated the loud, uninhibited girls bouncing off the wall for attention. He didn't complain or gossip about women who showed too much skin, but it just wasn't compelling to him. He preferred the nerdy girl who covered up her body and left more to the imagination.

A child of God or not, he always felt a glimpse, or a tease of hotness, was always more effective.

I had to really reach back in my archives to notice Leeann because she had changed so much. I'm not an all-knowing or all-seeing being like God. So sometimes I can be surprised at a person's change. You know! A Sunday School Teacher turned a crack head type of way.

But running into Leeann was a pleasant surprise for me, and I knew she would be perfect for Frank's demise.

Her coffee-chocolate skin and large, hazel brown eyes only enhanced her tantalizing, bright smile. She may have toned down her sexuality to find the perfect man, but I knew who she really was.

She looked flawless in every way on the outside, but her heart, mind, and soul were dissolute.

As soon as Frank saw Leeann in the campus library, I knew he could not resist her. She was receptive towards Frank's perspective of the bible, which was a striking contrast to everything and everyone around him.

He was immediately smitten by her confidence, beauty, and astuteness. They never officially dated or became a couple, but they were always spotted around campus together.

Frank genuinely enjoyed being around Leeann. They spent time watching movies, disclosed their dreams and aspirations to each other, worked out together, and on occasions sulked because they were angry at each other. But they always seemed to find their way back to each other.

Frank especially looked forward to the verbal chess playing, but most of all he cherished their time together.

Frank often wondered why she had not accepted Jesus Christ as her personal savior, and she would always respond with the same feisty response.

"It's a personal preference. Frank, I'll talk to you about anything else except having a personal relationship with Christ because it will end with you just throwing around a bunch of bible verses, and I know it's much more than that."

Her response always frustrated Frank because he was certain that he could change her mind about Christ if she would just listen.

Frank pressed the issue so much that one afternoon Leeann finally agreed to listen.

Frank's excitement showed as spoke in a passionate voice.

"Leeann, God knows everything about you and considers you incredibly valuable. We become children of God when we believe Jesus died for the sins of the world. He was crucified and shed his blood for you. Once you accept Christ, he dwells in us forever, and he will never leave or forsake you. Jesus Christ suffered for all the sins of the world, and in his death, we were baptized and resurrected in the body of Christ as heirs of his kingdom. Not a human being on earth can love as much or be as forgiving as God. His love is infinite... So, what do you say, are you ready to accept Christ?"

Leeann smiled at Frank and nodded her head in approval.

"Ok, I'm impressed! I still don't see how my life would change that much, but I'm impressed.

Frank leaned forward with excitement expecting the conversation to go further, as Leeann dropped her gaze and looked at her watch.

"Yikes! I didn't know it was getting that late. You can come back to my place if you want."

Frank was hesitant about being alone with Leeann because there was always the possibility of temptation.

"I'm not sure if that's a good idea, Leeann? You know! With my spiritual belief and all."

I spoke with Leeann about Frank's indecision, and like a savvy chess player catching a beginner opponent off guard, she made her move. She laughed at Frank and playfully punched him in the shoulder.

"You're a mess! I'm enjoying our conversation and you're worried about me tempting you? Trust me Frank. You're safe! I don't want you!"

She smiled with amusement as she studied his facial expressions. Then she playfully teased him with a low, disdainful voice.

"Tempting you? Wow! I didn't know you were God's gift to the world!"

She quickly shoved a pile of books into her backpack and walked toward the door.

An awkward grin slid across Frank's face as he grabbed his books, hurried behind her, and whispered in her direction.

"Leeann, Leeann, slow up! I didn't mean to offend you. I was just trying to avoid..."

He breathed a sigh of relief as she laughed at him, and he nervously held the door open and playfully blocked her progress at the same time.

"Frank, you're crazy! Get out my way!"

Frank smiled at her as the heavy door slammed shut behind them. He convinced himself that she wasn't trying to tempt him, but that she was just being herself. That's just who she was! That's what made her so attractive; she was feisty but modest.

It was cold outside with a drizzling rain falling from the gray sky. And Frank offered to share his umbrella with her. The night gloom soon faded to a dark-gray sky and the rain stopped just as they arrived at Leeann's dorm.

Leeann smiled at Frank and scanned her student ID card.

"You're really a good guy Frank, but it's not all about you all the time. Not everything is always about the church and the bible. Sometimes people just want to talk about regular stuff going on in their lives and have a good conversation. I'll see you around, Frank."

Leeann walked inside and Frank stepped back to allow the door to close.

As I stated before, my temptations are remarkably clever. Clever! But you can overcome them. I've learned that in all my years of setting snares and traps, Christ has always given his children a way out. Your way out might not always be as transparent as it should be, but there is always an escape route.

Frank foolishly ignored his escape route and allowed his curiosity to present an alternate picture.

I painted a picture of what Leeann thought of him. In his mind, he looked like a hypocrite. Leeann didn't say what she was thinking, but he had seen it on her face. She thought that he was naïve. That he was hiding behind the bible to avoid friendship and that when it came to discussions about anything except the bible, he was awkward and aloof. And that she was not important because she was not a Christian.

He timidly tapped on the door's glass just as Leeann disappeared through a second door. And Frank peered through the glass like a lonely puppy waiting for his owner to arrive.

Frank turned to walk away and remembered that he had Leeann's directory call number. He fumbled through his wallet, found the number, and sat quietly on the bench, contemplating if using the code was a wise thing for him.

This is always an anxious time for Christians because there is a battle between Christ and me. He wants you to leave the situation as soon as possible, so he starts giving you bible verses and attacking your conscience. He's trying to keep you at a safe distance from the fire and I want you smack in the middle of it.

This is the time during temptation that you don't just walk away, you run away! Walking gives you time to reconsider, to think about it a little longer. And when you're at that point in a situation, it's usually not a good place to be.

I submerge your senses with foresight and illusions of pleasure, or in Frank's case, I play on his compassionate spirit.

Frank was admittedly drawn to Leeann's beauty but chose to keep the attraction to himself. His faith in Christ kept his feelings about her tethered deep inside. It was far more important that she accept Jesus Christ into her life, than him having a meaningful relationship with her. On one hand, he wanted to explain to her that it was not his intention to hurt her. But, on the other hand, he knew being alone with her in her room was against everything he believed in. Frank did not see himself as a weak man succumbing to temptation at every corner, but his attraction to Leeann had grown over the past months. In the campus library, he was safe because everyone was watching. Alone, in her room! Now that was a different story.

No matter how many of these warning signs Christ gave him, I continued my attack on his compassion.

It's a little trick I learned over the years.

For Frank, I wanted his compassion to be polite, enabling, and passive. And to give Leeann a nod of approval to do what she wanted.

Frank stood up to leave because he had made up his mind. He had no idea what Leeann had in store for him in her room, and he did not want to find out. I wanted Frank in that room, and I was going to get him there by hook or crook.

He took one step in the opposite direction and I pounced on him.

"Frank, why are you treating this poor girl like that? The most effective way to minister to her is to offer her a message of hope, rather than judgement. Ultimately, it's the Holy Spirit who condemns, not you! She should know that you are a Christian by your love. But that won't happen if you come across as judgmental. If anything, that will chase her away from Christ. She doesn't need you to tell her that she's going to hell, she already knows that. What she needs is for you to show her that a different life is possible, regardless of the sin that she's trapped in. There's nothing wrong with talking with her in her room if you keep Jesus the focus of your conversation and outreach. Come on, Frank! You can do this! Go team Jesus!"

I didn't know if my little speech would work with Frank, because he was under such conviction to leave. Both Jesus and I gave Frank our best presentations.

And then I saw him turn and start walking towards the keypad. Jesus had given Frank every sign in the book, and still he listened to me.

I think deep down inside, Frank wanted to know if he and Leeann could be equally yoked. I could have answered that question for him, but who am I to keep a curious mind locked away.

Frank punched in Leeann's room code and nervously tapped the box. Frank keyed the code a second time after seeing someone peek out a third-floor window and immediately heard the excitement in Leeann's voice as the door latch popped from locked to open.

Frank quickly walked through the door and trotted up the steps towards the second floor. He looked up and saw Leeann smiling at him while looking over the banister.

"Hey Frank! Come on up! You have to excuse my clothes because I wasn't expecting anyone."

Frank stopped abruptly and responded.

"I can leave if you're busy or come back a different day?"

Frank was hoping that she would say yes so that he could run out of the building.

"No! Come on up Frank. I was just listening to some music and ordering some stuff off Amazon."

Frank followed Leeann up the stairs and down a dimly lit corridor. He felt a lump in his throat as he walked into her dorm room, and he already regretted the decision to come up to her room. Her University of Cincinnati T-shirt had been cut off just below her bust, and her gym shorts fit snugly around her perfect thighs. Her scented body wash smelled like orange sherbet and vanilla, and his mouth watered because she smelled good enough to taste. She leaned forward to turn off her laptop, and her tiny shorts slid upward, revealing the curve of her butt.

She sat on her bed, rested her back against the wall, and invited Frank to sit in the office chair which she had pulled near her bed. Frank quickly sat down and wheeled the chair backward to create an invisible barrier.

Leeann crossed her legs Indian style and leaned forward. She rested her face on her hands and her elbows on her knees and studied Frank's facial expressions intently.

"So Frank, what's up?"

Frank's eyes squinted as he tried hard to keep his eyes focused on Leeann's face, but it was hard. The way her legs were positioned gave Frank the perfect view of seeing her smooth inner thighs meeting at her perfectly, sexy, chocolate V. The thought of sliding in and out of her had him fully erect as he stammered to answer her.

"Well, Leeann, I was just wondering. I mean, I just wanted to clear the air with us and make sure we were still cool. I don't want you to think that we can't be friends just because I'm a Christian and you're not. I enjoy our conversations, and I think about you a lot! I mean, I care about what you think of me."

Frank shook his head and sighed heavily as he appeared frustrated at what he was trying to say.

Leeann did not help matters, because all she did was stare at him with an adorable smirk on her face. Either she didn't realize that she was enticing him with her pelvic area or she knew and just didn't care. Frank was praying for the former because he was now unsure if he could avoid falling for the latter.

But I already knew what Leeann's intentions were.

I had convinced Frank that Leeann was nothing more than an innocent person in need of and seeking Christ. While Frank was playing Christian checkers, Leeann was five steps ahead of him playing temptation chess. While Frank was walking around outside, debating if he should run away from Leeann's dorm, she was showering and preparing for when he inevitably came back. I had set Frank up with the old double move. Even if he had run home, Leeann would have called him and convinced him to come back to discuss any differences. It just so happened that Frank fell for the poor, lost, compassionate, soul first.

Leeann never saw Frank as a boyfriend and husband because she could not be close to any man beyond a game of sexual conquest.

I planted this seed in her years ago through her selfish parents and Julius. What if her father, John, had resisted temptation and stayed in his daughter's life to guide her? What if Leeann's mother had chosen the safety of her daughter over alcohol and the lure of Julius' money? Would that have given her the capacity to see beyond Frank as being just a sexual conquest?

It's not my fault when things go wrong! I don't force you to do anything; I just create the circumstances by tempting you. You might think of it as cruel, but the responsible people in Leeann's life should have known what their choices would result in.

Leeann was the perfect temptress for Frank's downfall. She was almost machine-like with her feelings, warm and engaging one minute, and cold and calculating the next. She only cared about her selfish needs, and her needs at that moment were to have a man committed to Christ submit to her desires. She wanted to turn everything that made him great into something evil and vile for her own personal gratitude.

Leeann's eyes appeared to be anxious, almost wishing that Frank would ask for what he wanted. She uncrossed her legs, moved to the edge of the bed, and in one quick motion, pulled Frank's chair towards her. Frank immediately tensed up. Her legs were spread wide and Frank sat motionless, with his hands folded in front of him. The smell of vanilla grew stronger as she pulled the chair closer and scooted her body closer to him. Frank could feel the warmth of Leeann's vagina as he strained to keep his fingers curled into a fist.

Leeann looked down at his hands and dissolved into laughter as she fell backward on the bed.

"You are so cute! You don't have to be afraid; I'm not going to bite you."

Frank pushed the chair back almost in anger and started walking towards the door.

"I told you that I can't be doing this! I need to get out of here."

Leeann bounced from the bed and grabbed Frank by the arm. Frank was moving so fast that he stumbled backward against the door and fell into Leeann's embrace.

Her body felt warm and she smelled so delicious. Frank wanted to push her off and run, but his arms were weak, and his legs felt like jelly. He tried to push her away, but his hand mistakenly touched her butt. He quickly moved his hand away and froze as if he had gotten caught stealing candy. Leeann grabbed his wrist and slowly guided his hand back towards her butt. She held his hand there until he no longer had the will to fight. His arm relaxed and his hand gently cupped one of her soft cheeks. Her body moved closer to him and he felt his manhood aching to be released. She slowly moved forward, and her soft lips gently touched his. She stared into his eyes and whispered,

"You can't do this with me! Or are you afraid of what you will feel if you do this with me."

Frank felt ashamed of what he was feeling and refused to return her gaze. He looked in every direction except in her eyes. He wanted to break away, but the warmth and softness of her body held him captive. The more he massaged her body, the more desire he had for her.

"Leeann please, this is wrong! I can't do this. I'm afraid of what can happen."

Leeann pulled Frank closer and gently nibbled on his neck while rubbing her body against his. Her body movement was not wild or out of control, it was shifting almost rhythmically against him. Frank had never felt anything like this before. Her body was almost comforting; enticing him to do whatever he wanted to her. She placed his hand inside her shorts and allowed him to caress and gently fondle her. She felt warm as his fingers slid around her softness until finally sinking inside her.

She moaned with approval and lifted one leg up so that he could explore as he pleased. Her sounds of passion, warmth, and moistness were driving Frank out of his mind. He had never been in a position like this before because he was a virgin.

He had watched a couple of porn scenes on his phone and pleasured himself. But he had no idea what he should do. He knew that Leeann was ready to go further, but he was confused about what he should do. Should he pick her up like a caveman and throw her on the bed. Or should he continue rubbing and playing inside her.

Leeann lowered her leg and slowly pulled him towards her bed. Frank gave no resistance as his body limply staggered towards her. She fell backward on the bed pulling Frank on top of her. Her legs spread apart, and her lower body invited Frank to continue their slow grind on the bed. Frank was intrigued by the way her body was responding to his movement. When he pushed himself against her at a certain angle, her body would shiver, and she would sigh with passion.

Frank's fascination quickly turned to fear when Leeann tugged at the belt attached to his pants.

"Hold on Leeann! Please, I must tell you something. Please Leeann stop!"

Frank grabbed Leeann's hands and held them tightly to keep her from pulling his pants off, and Leeann discontinued her assault.

"Leeann, I am attracted to you, but I can't do this. I love God, and besides, I have never done this before. I was saving myself for my wife. I can't do this Leeann because I'm a virgin."

Leeann smiled at Frank as if he were a child telling her the truth when caught lying. His eyes were round with fear as he waited for her reaction. Frank was sure that Leeann would laugh and kick him out of her room. A twenty-four-year-old virgin with a bible complex! Oh yeah! He was getting kicked out with the quickness. Frank thought that it would probably be good if she did kick him out; it would almost be like God was saving him.

I know that's what Frank wished for, but my plans for him were the total opposite. Frank's big day at church was just two days away, and I needed his downfall to be messy. I wanted his pastor, congregation, and parents watching as the great Frank Barkley tumbled from God's grace. Leeann would probably never amount to anything except for a good bed partner, but on that cold, rainy night, she was Satan's MVP.

She was the only person that could convince Frank that leaving Christ was in his best interest. The only other woman that I had seen with more deceitfulness in her heart was Delilah.

When Samson's big ass woke up and couldn't bust a grape, it was like winning the Olympics.

And Frank giving in to temptation on the weekend he was scheduled to be ordained as an Elder would be just as big.

Leeann pulled Frank close and he rested his head on her chest. She embraced him lovingly like a mother almost comforting him like a kid.

"Frank, I think it's so sweet that you are keeping yourself for your future wife. I think you will make an amazing husband. I just have one question! What makes you think that your future wife is not in your life right now?"

She held him even tighter and gently rubbed his back. Frank responded by wrapping his arms around her waist and pulling her closer. Frank was very confused about what he was feeling. He had always asked God to send him a good, God-fearing woman. And in his current state of mind, here she was!

In Frank's eyes, Leeann was a good woman. She was smart, articulate, great looking, almost everything he had dreamed. The missing piece was God-fearing.

Frank knew that she was leading him away from Christ, but he was sure he could change her. At least he was certain before. Now he was in conflict with himself about what he should do.

Leeann continued her seduction of Frank and eventually broke him.

"Frank, I would never force you to do anything that you didn't feel comfortable doing. You have been such a stable presence in my life these past few months, and I don't want to throw it all away. I've never been around a man who gave so much to me and never asked for anything in return. My father walked out of my life when I was young, and my mother and I are always at odds with each other. There's something about your spirit that brings such peace to me. You deserve this night! And I want to be that special person for you forever. I don't have much to offer you, but I do know that I care for you more than I should. I knew it was foolish of me to fall for you, knowing that you would probably never see me as that special person in your life, but I'm past that now. Your faith will probably never allow us to be together, and I understand that. But I'm still willing to take that chance. I'm not asking you for a lifetime; I'm just asking you for tonight."

Frank could feel his face getting warm, and his eyes became blurry with tears. His thoughts were in disarray as he tried to decide what he should do.

Standing on the word and staying true to God should have been an easy choice. But I don't give easy choices. I make it hard for you with multiple choice answers. You can stay true to your faith but lose a damn good woman. You can stand on the word and miss what you're feeling right now. Or you can sit in your lonely apartment and pray to God for another twenty-four years.

I could see Frank's mind slowly working through his dilemma, so I helped him decide.

Leeann slowly slid her hand down Frank's chest and stomach. Her hand came to a stop on his penis. She gently massaged it until he had no fight left in him. His hands slid away from her wrist, allowing her to unbuckle his pants. Frank was nervous and his body was trembling from the unknown. Leeann slithered out of her tiny t-shirt revealing her perky breasts; and climbed onto Frank's lap. Frank instinctively grabbed for them like an out of control animal. His grip was so firm and aggressive that Leeann jerked away in pain.

"Ouch! Calm down baby! You don't have to be in a rush; we have all night to be together." Here, let me show you."

She pulled his hand back towards her breast and slowly rubbed it with her nipple. He had heard guys on campus talking about sucking on a girl's breast and decided to give it a try. He placed his mouth around one of her breasts and began sucking hard like he was drinking the last drop of water from a bottle in the desert. Again, Leeann pulled away, gently stroking his back.

"Uh-huh baby, softly."

Again, she thrust her breast in Frank's face and he eagerly slurped at her breast like an ice cream cone on a hot summer day. He was amazed at the way her nipples stiffened, and her body swayed back and forth with approval. She placed her hand on Frank's chest and shoved him backward on the bed and stood on the floor. She slowly peeled out of the tight shorts and smiled as Frank's eyes danced across her body with contentment. Leeann leaned her body over Frank and began to kiss him. Her soft touches enhanced his hunger for her as she undressed him. Frank was unsure of what he should do, but with each kiss and each touch, he saw the uncertainty vanish.

Leeann straddled him with an intense enticement in her eyes. His hands landed on her hips as he held his breath. She teased him by hovering over his hard penis, subtly touching the engorged head. He had to be inside her. He wanted to feel her warm slick walls gliding against him. Her teasing only enhanced his hunger for her as she leaned forward with a seductive smile, whispering, in between kisses.

"What do you want?"

Frank was shivering from her touches, and he appeared out of breath from the excitement.

"You, I got to have you right here, right now. Please!"

Leeann smiled as she lowered her hips, allowing him to push deep inside her. He moaned in ecstasy as she rocked her hips. With each movement of her hips, Frank found it hard to control himself. The gratification in Leeann's eyes made Frank want to prod deeper inside her. The soft, warm, slickness was even more intense then he could have ever imagined. Frank strained to keep himself tight, but he felt himself slowly trickling inside her. He had heard people talk about thinking about other things like baseball during sex, but he was having a hard time focusing. He turned his head sideways and tried to center his attention on the dim desk light, but it was of no use.

Leeann leaned forwarded and whispered, "Frank! I want all of you inside me." Her walls clamped around him, and her hips began to swivel at a rapid pace. Frank's body stiffened and his face shifted into a contorted grimace. It was like something from deep inside him had erupted, and it was forcefully surging forward. The ecstasy of his orgasm was so vigorous that his body continued to twitch uncontrollably even as her body melted around him. They stayed wrapped in each other's arms, breathing heavily, with Leeann lying on his chest. Leeann lifted her head and kissed Frank slowly, purposely. Frank wasn't sure what had just happened to him, but he was certain that it was powerful. He didn't have time to think about it at that moment, but when she gazed into his eyes, he knew, somehow, someway, she would always have a special place in his heart.

He should have felt afraid and guilty, but he didn't. Lying in the dimly lit room holding Leeann close felt so right, and nothing in the world mattered at that moment. He didn't care that he had missed church services he just wanted to hold on to what he was feeling.

"Frank! That was so special and amazing for me. I can lay right here, with you, for the rest of my life. This is that feeling that I've always been searching for."

She rolled to Frank's side and allowed him to hold her from behind. She pushed her buttocks against him again, playfully spooning with him. Frank felt out of control because his body reacted to the slightest movement of her body. Leeann inspired Frank to enter a cocoon of pleasure that lasted all through the night. Even when morning arrived, Frank still refused to separate himself from his newly found paradise. He spent the morning, and most of the day, making love and wrapped in a blanket with Leeann watching TV. When they finally decided to leave the room for something to eat, it was past dinner.

His heart was beating a million miles an hour. He could not believe the way he was feeling.

Was this how love felt?

If so, he never wanted to be without it again. There was an animal magnetism between them that was inextinguishable. More than that, there was a deep connection happening that he never knew existed.   What happened between them was not planned or calculated; it just happened.

They left the restaurant and walked to a nearby park. The city was literally glistening around them. The crowds bellowing from nearby shops, restaurants, and bars seemed far away. He was aware of these things, but they seemed muffled and the more they talked, the more everything melted into the background. The whole world could have caught fire and Frank would have never known.

Damn Frank! She really put that thang on you!

After walking in the park, Frank found himself back in Leeann's room making love again.

It was like Frank could not get enough of her. Everything about her was so impulsive and exciting. All the stories he had heard from

Elders and Bishops about how a woman could take you away from God was now his reality.

All Frank could see himself doing was waiting patiently for Leeann to mystify him with one impassioned technique after another. He felt like a caveman discovering fire over and over. Everything she did made him cum harder than the previous time.

Now he understood perfectly how his father could walk away from Christ, especially if it made him feel this good.

By the time she finally fell asleep in his arms, he was resigned to the fact that his relationship with Christ was over, and he was perfectly satisfied with that. As long as Leeann could continue to give him a teeny portion of what she had given him the past couple of days, he was willing to throw his faith away.

Frank woke up in the middle of the night restless, and Leeann slept serenely beside him. Leeann's spell of lustful temptation had subsided, and all he could do was stare at the ceiling trying to make sense of his decisions over the past two days.

The fear and regret of his choices caused his ears to ring with white noise, and he was hurting from a lack of sleep. It was like he was waking up from a spring break, alcohol bender, with regrets.

All those nights that his father paced the floor at night and mumbled like a madman. This had to be how it all starts!

When Frank left for college, he remembered the conversation that his father had with him about holding on to God's unchanging hand.

"No matter what temptation Satan's throws in your direction seek God first, and never allow anyone or anything to separate you from the Love of God."

At the time, Frank did not take those words seriously. All he could hear was a bunch of gibberish coming from a hypocrite. He never realized how true that statement was until he was lying, curled up, next to one of Satan's imps.

His phone was full of urgent text messages from his pastor, mother, and concerned church members. He had missed the gospel concert on Friday night, and now he had missed the Saturday youth praise service. Frank got up enough courage to send a group text message indicating that he had a last-minute research paper, and then he turned his phone off. Most people who knew Frank probably knew it was untrue because he never did anything last minute.

He, along with four other ministers had been tapped by the Bishop to be ordained as Elders, and he was the headliner.

The ceremony at St. Stephens was huge. In fact, the entire week leading up to the Ordination service was huge. The week is labeled the Youth Conference Convention. The young members of the church invite their family and friends to participate in daily themed events during the week. The four candidates slated to be ordained are selected to bring forth God's word on their chosen night. The Bishop, along with the Elders of the church, paid close attention to these sermonettes. The most creative and passionate minister was chosen to close out the convention on Sunday. It was like everybody had been hearing all these great things about you all week, and now you were live and in color.

Frank's sermonette occurred on Thursday night. And although it's not a competition, it was safe to say that he gave the most fervent message of the four. His deep, rich, stentorian voice resonated across the large church filled with young impressionable minds. His voice was like warm syrup for their fledgling souls, as he warned them about me stealing their joy.

"God wants your Spirit to be peaceful. He wants you to feel comfortable and full of joy because He knows that when your emotional bucket is full, it's easier to accomplish your spiritual mission, which is to glorify Him, and spread his Love. But Satan doesn't want that! I don't think you heard me saints, Satan does not want that!   He wants to steal your joy, so that all your focus turns inward to all the things that are wrong in your life. Satan loves for you to feel guilty and afraid. He wants you to lust after those beautiful men and women in your DM, so that you will be thinking about having a sexual encounter, rather than shining your light for others to see. When you begin to feel that lustful Spirit flooding your soul, remember, it isn't really that person or that situation that is causing your discomfort. It's Satan, the original power of darkness. He's trying to steal your joy; He's trying to dim your light. He wants you to give into your sinful desires and sin. And if you do, Satan will have won! Don't let Satan win! Don't let him take you away from God's Love. When you feel your Spirit start to sink and you keep replaying all those lustful images in your mind, ask God to refocus your thoughts. Lust, evil desires, and sexual frustration are not from God. Put up your hand and say, "No! I am not having it that way. I am choosing to focus on Christ's love and keeping my peace." By only focusing on positive, kind, loving thoughts, you give Satan no opportunity to enter your mind. With God's help, you can reclaim your joy and get back to the business of doing those things that he created you to do."

Frank even had his rivals applauding his auditory skills and his message of hope. How ironic that his message was a warning about my deceptions and snares, and he ended up stuck in one.

Frank woke up early on Sunday looking for the best solution. His dilemma was complicated, because the essence of everything that made him spiritual was riding on his ordination. Becoming an ordained Elder had been the single most desired objective in his life since he had given his life to Christ. Overseers of the church were amazed at how young he was, but yet able to still deliver God's message with such power and authority. Most of the congregation at St. Stephens Pentecostal Church had witnessed many people saved through his teachings as a youth minister. As a matter of fact, twenty people, including a twelve-year-old girl, had given their lives to God during his Thursday night sermonette.

Frank sat on the side of Leeann's bed with his head buried in his hands as if he had a hangover. He felt worthless and miserable; what a difference two days had made!

Thursday night was filled with praise, worship, and sanctification. And during the qualifications interview, he had proudly sat in front of the church. The Bishop and council of six members, had asked questions and the congregation responded, "Above reproach."

It sounded like a call and response at a pep rally.

"Article one, Blameless?"

"Above reproach."

"Article two, Vigilant?"

"Above reproach."

 "Article three, Sober?"

"Above reproach."

 "Article four, given to hospitality?"

"Above reproach."

"Article five, apt to teach?"

"Above reproach."

Article six, holding fast the faithful word as he has been taught, that he may be able by sound doctrine both to exhort and to convict the gainsayers."

"Above reproach."

"Article seven, not given to wine, patient, not a brawler, not angry?"

"Above reproach."

"Article eight, not given to filth, lust, not covetous?"

"Above reproach."

Therefore, brethren, pick out from among you men of good repute, full of the Spirit and of wisdom, whom we may appoint to this duty. Elders should be peacemakers, prayer warriors, teachers, leaders by example, and decision-makers. They are the preaching and teaching leaders of the church. It is a position to be sought but not taken lightly—read this warning: "Let not many of you become teachers, my brethren, for you know that we who teach shall be judged with greater strictness. The role of the elder is not a position to be taken lightly."

The congregation replied with thunderous applause and praised God for sending them a holy man.

It was an amazing feeling!

Now all he could feel was guilt from his betrayal. He contemplated not going, but that would only make matters worse. Everybody was going to be present for his ordination. Older members in the church had prophesied about this day, and now it was here. Students and professors from the University's Theology Department had been invited and RSVP'd. His parents, as well as other members of the church community, were coming.

He had no choice; he had to show!

Entry:
Failed Project

Leeann looked beautiful lying in bed. Her body was partially covered with a sheet, and the uncovered portion was enough to give a normal man an early morning erection. But not Frank! Frank was in no mood for sexual favors. All he could do was think about the guilt of his transgression.

I know how he felt because I've seen the same old story thousands of times, from Adam and Eve in the garden to the endless church affairs. It's like a hamster on his little wheel. Guilt creates fear, and fear makes you sin, and sin makes you guilty, and the guilt makes you afraid, and so you sin again to escape more guilt and fear. It's the human condition, the original sin of thinking that God will abandon you, and not let you back into his grace because you once ate a piece of fruit.

Frank took a deep breath and leaned over to kiss Leeann. He would have preferred that she continue to sleep, but his sudden presence startled her. She yawned and smiled at Frank. Her voice was heavy with weighty exhaustion.

"Hey baby! You're up early."

Frank managed a partial smile as he responded with regret in his voice.

"Yeah, I have to run over to the church really quick and unlock the doors. I promised the pastor that I would do that, but I will call you later."

Frank was hoping that he could give Leeann a quick alibi and scurry out.

Leeann rubbed her eyes so that she could focus on Frank's face. She lifted her neck and studied his face briefly as if searching for something, and then lowered her head back on the pillow with interest in her voice, "Um hum!"

Frank felt like Leeann did not buy his story, so he began to downplay where he was going.

"I don't know why the Bishop only trusts me to unlock the doors because he has deacons. I think he wants me to get more involved with the deacons so that I understand their duties more."

Leeann raised her body and placed a pillow behind her back for support. She glared at Frank as if she were annoyed with him.

"If you don't want me to come to your event, just say it! You don't have to lie about what you're doing Frank! You're not a child, and I'm not your mother."

Frank wanted to argue his point, and in fact he should have. But he chose to appease Leeann's growing anger and lie.

"No, no, no! It's not that, Leeann. I would love for you to go, but I didn't think you wanted to go. Plus, the services can be super long, and I have to stay for the 3:30 and 7:00 services. Seriously baby! You really don't want to get caught up in those long services. They go on and on and on. Just stay here and I will swing by later and we can do something."

Frank quickly put on his jogging pants, as Leeann sat on the bed looking bitter, with resentment in her eyes. Frank gave a quick wave of the hand and exited the small dorm room.

As I said before, guilt creates fear, and fear makes you sin again. Frank is normally a good person, but that morning he was in panic. He didn't care if he was hurting Leeann's feelings. In his mind, he was running away from me and my temptations, what he should have really done in the first place.

If he could just make it through the day, he would be ok. He felt guilty for what he had done the past two days. He felt guilty for lying to his pastor. And above all, he felt guilty because he was now transgressing against God.

He ran to his dorm room and quickly showered. He threw on the same suit, shirt, and tie that he had worn during Thursday's service because he never got a chance to get his clothes out of the dry cleaners.

I tell you, when you Christians fall off the horse, you fall hard!

Frank's thoughts were racing a hundred miles per hour as he hurried to his car. He had already missed the prayer breakfast, and now he was in danger of missing the procession of the candidates.

This was the only Sunday that he would get the opportunity to enter the church leading the procession. The normal order of the procession was: Choir, visiting clergy, resident clergy, Ordained Elders, and finally, the Bishop.

For this one Sunday, the four candidates replaced the choir, and Frank would lead the entire procession to the pulpit.

And up until two days ago, Frank was excited. Now, he was looking for any excuse to not even show for the ceremony.

I arrived early because this was going to be "can't miss entertainment." I saw several ushers darting in and out of the large crowd assembled in the church's foyer. The head usher was an overweight, dark-skinned woman with a short frizzy afro. She was organizing people in their correct line position, while cackling and gossiping with the choir director, Fredrick. He was a good-looking man, with black, curling hair, tampered into a fade. He had on a smart man-tailored suit and his movements were exaggerated and feminine.

When I saw Fredrick, I immediately smiled to myself because I knew of his work. Fredrick enjoyed gossiping. His phone calls, text messages, and social media were filled with gossip. He gossiped about his family, friends, and everybody in the church. All of his friends only talked to him because he knew all the latest gossip. His latest gossip involved Frank being seen last night at a restaurant, with a Jezebel-looking woman instead of being at church service.

I straightaway put my plan in motion, just as Frank's car was screeching to halt in the parking lot.

Leeann never had any intention of staying cooped up in her room. As a matter of fact, as soon as Frank left the room, I had a conversation with her pride.

"What type of shit is that? You gave him a very special part of you last night, and that's the thanks you get? Wam, Bam, thank you mam! Anybody else would have given their left arm just to be in your presence, and this church boys got the nerve to treat you like this. You're worth more than that! You deserve more than that! Julius did it to you! Alvin did it to you! And now you're letting a church boy do you the same way. Girl, what has your life really come to."

Me pressing Leeann's buttons, along with her missing a couple of days of medication can cause a lot of confusion. Poor Frank and Leeann didn't have a fighting chance against me.

I know what you're saying, "Satan, it's your fault! You're the author of confusion and blah-blah-blah."

Hold on! Slow your roll! Let's talk truth. I may manipulate and maneuver you into doing wrong or having envious thoughts, but only you can allow it. My job is to divide and separate you in some form or fashion from God. I convince you to feel like someone did you wrong because I need you to be at odds with that person. Any problems that I can stir up between people only benefits me because it leads to confusion. Confusion destroys you spiritually and emotionally, and it steals your joy. It's impossible to be bitter towards someone and have inner peace at the same time. If you really want me to leave you alone, have a forgiving spirit.

Leeann began digging out of the back of the closet, and her eyes narrowed as she found what she was looking for. She held up a black and white pinstripe sundress and smiled with amusement. She matched the dress perfectly with sexy, thong- undergarments, and a pair of high heel gladiator stilettoes. The sight was amazing!

The dress pressed tightly against every curve of her body, and it was so short that it barely covered her very shapely behind. The slightest movement made it wiggle and bounce to the enjoyment of the boys gathered on fraternity row.

She jumped into her Nissan Maxima and sped toward St. Stephens Pentecostal. She hoped that the skintight ensemble would raise eyes long enough to achieve her goal. In her mind, he was either going to love her, hate her, or be humiliated by her. And if humiliation was his choice, that dress made her well prepared. She had no problem walking in the ceremony and exposing who Frank had been with for the past two days.

"Yeah, that's right Bishop! Your favorite candidate has been all up in my pussy for the past two days. I'm sorry mama Barkley, but your baby came inside me so hard that he almost passed out!"

Leeann was still finalizing scenarios in her mind as she pulled into the parking lot. The choir had just finished singing and the procession was about to start when Leeann opened the door. Frank was quietly speaking with the other candidates when he saw Leeann walking towards him.   He looked shocked-not happy or unhappy, simply shocked. She smiled at him and congratulated him, and despite his apparent discomfort, he remained calm. He shook her hand and thanked her for attending. For all anyone knew, Leeann could have been just a friend attending his big day.

Leeann quickly put the 'just a friend' notion to rest just as the ushers opened the foyer doors. She grabbed Frank and seductively pressed her body against his while hugging. She nuzzled his cheek so passionately that the ushers contemplated closing the door back. The congregation peered at Leeann and Frank, dumbfounded by what they were seeing. After a long embrace, she pulled back and gently kissed his lips while whispering.

"I'm so proud of you, baby!"

The uncomfortable rustling in the church sanctuary suddenly changed to an awkward silence.

Leeann slowly made her way toward the front of the church. As she walked by the gallery of deacons, their mouths opened in unison, as if they were having a hard time breathing. The silk dress was clinging to her hips as her body swayed suggestively. Her breasts were peeking over the top of the sundress, like creamy, chocolate mounds. She looked over her shoulder, fully aware of the effect she was having on them and smiled. Leeann sat in the pew in front of Frank's mother, and she frowned as if she smelled something awful. The congregation mumbled to each other and shifted in their seats uncomfortably.

Frank began the long walk down the aisle as the procession reluctantly followed. He looked guilty; he felt guilty. In fact, he looked guilty and miserable. When he stood at the lectern he wobbled slightly. He looked awed, stunned, and embarrassed. He wanted to say something, but nothing was coming forward. There was an uncomfortable silence that appeared to go on and on.

Finally, the silence was broken by Fredrick when he scoffed in a comically bemused tone.

"Girrrl, I just know he didn't do what I think he did!"

Other people in the audience began to snicker at what Fredrick was saying. A lot of people were thinking about it, but they were too embarrassed to say it out loud.

Fredrick folded his arms against his chest and raised his eyebrows with a girl-I-told-you-so look.

He rocked back and forth with exaggerated feminine gestures, mumbling loud enough so that his cronies in his gossip club could hear.

"Uh huh girl … this ahh sin, and ahh shame. This man done brought something like this in God's house."

Muffled giggles echoed throughout the choir as Frank began to shake visibly. Leeann, sensing that Fredrick was talking about her, quickly stood to her feet and responded.

"Little faggot! You better watch who you're talking to?"

Fredrick's demeanor went from humorous to utter surprise. He was taken aback by her crude comment and took a moment to look at her. Everyone knew that Fredrick was gay, but no one had ever stated it out loud and in such a venomous manner.

Fredrick's face contorted into a mask of fury, his eyes narrowed, and he pointed a finger in Leeann's direction.

"You're a whore! Everything about you screams Backpage!

Annoyed by Fredrick, Leeann began to slowly move in his direction almost as if she were stalking prey. Four deacons quickly rushed towards Leeann and grabbed her. Leeann was screaming at the top of her lungs.

"Get the fuck off me!"

And Fredrick continued his visceral attack as several deacons and ushers were removing Leeann. Leeann was definitely out of control, but Fredrick was like gasoline being thrown on a four-alarm fire.

"Girl Bye! Go back to your pimp harlot! You need to be praying to God when you on them rusty knees, instead sucking di…"

The Bishop shoved Frank aside and screamed into the microphone in an attempt to regain control of the congregation.

"Ok everybody, let's calm down! The deacons and ushers are handling the situation."

But his message had fallen on deaf ears. The audience had turned into a school of frenzied sharks, in the middle of a pile of bloody gossip chum. People began moving about freely trying to find out what was going on. A large group was gathered around Fredrick trying to calm him down, but he was insisting on telling them what he believed had occurred between Frank and Leeann.

"Why would anyone bring someone into the house God like that? You should have love and compassion for the sinner, but uh huh girl! She was doing too much."

I sat motionless and listened with a sort of patronizing smile. Joy and contentment were aching to come out, but I refused to show it.

If I had jumped up and screamed, "Hey Jesus! How you like me now, motherfucker?"

Someone would have certainly known who I was.

But this was absolutely everything I wanted to happen. I didn't think it would be so intense, but wow! This was definitely a victory for me.

I looked at Fredrick with admiration as he cried and begged the Bishop for forgiveness.

As I stated earlier, I knew Fredrick because of his works. He was no one special, but like Leeann, he was infested with the nastiest, most disgusting, cunning, and seductive spirit in my arsenal.

Jezebel!

Many people who hear about a Jezebel spirit, conjure up ideas of a seductive woman dressed scantily, trying to lure a man into a sexual tryst.

In reality, most people who have this type of spirit operate much more demurely than that. And most Bishops and pastors are not clued-up enough to spot this spirit, even when it's operating in their congregation. This spirit is a master at twisting the truth, lying, and blaming others for things instead of being honest.

They are very demanding and controlling, and they manipulate you by making you feel sorry for them or to make you feel indebted to them. I had planted Fredrick at St. Stephens many years ago, and his works within that church had gone unrestricted.

Not once had a mother, Elder, or Bishop ever challenged why a person with such a destructive spirit, had been allowed to roam so freely in that church. Sunday after Sunday, he manipulated, harassed, and gossiped about members at St. Stephens, and people simply passed it off as him being a messy, gay, Choir Director.

News flash Christians, being gay has absolutely nothing to do with having a Jezebel Spirit. People who operate in the spirit of Jezebel always have similar characteristics, whether they are a woman or a man. And let me be the first to tell you! If you leave Jezebel unchecked, she will not only tear down churches and pastors. She will break up marriages, friendships, and flat out get a person killed.

By the time St. Stephens Pentecostal knew what had hit them, I had released two Jezebel spirits inside of God's house. And they were causing so much chaos and disorder that the Bishop was contemplating shutting down the service.

Frank looked absolutely shell shocked. He could not believe that he had been deceived by Satan, in the form of the beautiful Leeann. I threw him one of the oldest curveballs in my arsenal, but it had so many layers that he never saw the attack coming.

I knew Jesus was probably upset because I had caught one of his faithful servants slipping. And God! Oh, my goodness! He probably was enraged at what I had done.

He probably already had Frank's name written in lights on Heavenly Boulevard, and here he was plummeting off his pedestal. I was elated at the sight of his pitiful face. He buried his face deep in his hands and began to wail and moan like he was at a funeral. Tears were streaming down his face, and every inch of his body shook with anguish. That embarrassment, guilt, and regret was tearing a hole in his heart, and there was nothing he could do to make the feeling go away. The rest of the congregation just stared at him silently, not knowing what to say or do in a situation like this. Frank's mother went to him and hugged him while whispering softly to him.

Stay strong baby, stay strong. God knows your heart.

Frank hugged his mother's waist tight and continued to cry. His face remained hidden in her stomach as if he were ashamed.

I looked at Frank and shook my head in amazement. I sighed and muttered to myself.

"This is sad! The ordination service of the celebrated Frank Barkley had turned into a deceitful mess."

And I loved it!

The way I turned such an organized commemoration of God's newest servant into chaotic disorder.

And most importantly, I had twisted and turned Frank's mind into a Rubik's cube of confusion, and he had no clear pathway back to God. His guilt and humiliation were so great that all he could manage to do was attempt to burrow his way back into his mother's womb.

If only Frank would have followed the template that Jesus used to vanquish my lures.

My temptation of Christ was a masterful array of enticements that were meant to challenge him mentally, spiritually, and physically.

He was afraid, hungry, and discouraged because he had been fasting for forty days searching for the strength to complete God's mission and save mankind.

My objective was to prevent that from ever occurring. I had to find a way to break his will! Find something weak within him that would give me an upper hand! I wanted to be able to get inside Jesus' head, the same way I got inside Eve's.

In the final hours before the cross, I had to persuade him somehow to follow me and leave mankind to perish.

I saw the desolation and gloom begin to slowly cloud Christ's vision as I whispered in his ear.

"Why in God's name would you want to save them. Every time God has given them a chance, they end up doing the same things. Look at Eve, look at Noah, look at Sodom and Gomorrah! Every time! And now God wants to sacrifice you to help them out."

I shook my head in disgust and tempted his human desire to eat.

"Damn, bro, I know you're hungry! You got to be hungry. You haven't eaten in forty days and your ribs are damn near touching. I would at least turn a couple of these rocks into Popeye's chicken sandwiches before you keel over and die from starvation."

Do you know what that prick had the nerve to say?

"Man does not live on bread alone but on every word that comes from the mouth of the Lord."

I laughed it off, but he was kind of making me angry with all that God said this and God said that, and it showed when I responded.

"What do you think God will do if I beat the fuck out of you? Better yet, what would happen if you jumped off this canyon? God would probably send a couple of angels to swoop you up before you hit the ground, hah! Well, I tell you what! Why don't we just test that theory and see what happens? I bet you'll bust your melon all over that valley down there. Oh, my bad! I forgot you're probably too chicken shit to do that, hah!"

Again he refused, mumbling about not wanting to abuse his powers to save himself.

I can't even lie; he had my anger level on DEFCON red. I was doing everything I could not to risk it all and murder that motherfucker. So, I came back with the ultimate offer.

"Look bro, we don't have to keep going back and forth with all this bullshit. You got a kingdom; I got a kingdom. But I can guarantee yours is not as big as mine. I'm not trying to flash on you, but no matter how far you look, I own it! Earth, Mars, Venus, I own all that shit! These humans just rent it! And if you play your cards right, you can have it all. All you have to do is give me your loyalty, and we will rule both heaven and earth. Instead of being a sacrificial lamb for mortals, you'll be an uncompromising wolf like me."

I saw the gears in his head turning, trying to weigh the odds. But in the end, he decided to remain strong. I guess the cost would have been too great. Jesus would have gained the world, but he would have given up his redemptive act of the crucifixion.

I tried my best to suppress his will to remain strong and deliver humanity, but he never flinched.

On the other hand, there was Frank!

That boy was sinking into the depths of depression like the Titanic. Just an ugly, crying, drooling mess! People were quickly losing all respect for him, and I was elated.

Suddenly, I noticed a plain, ordinary, almost weird-looking girl staring at me. At first, I thought she had overheard me, but I noticed that she was sitting three rows in front of me, and no one near me was looking in my direction. The entire congregation was facing forward looking at Frank and his mother. Everyone that is, except the little girl!

Her face was expressionless, and her large brown eyes were blank.

She peered at me curiously, like she knew me. Then the stare became cold and hard like she knew my spirit and it was too vile for that service. I glared back at her, and our eyes were locked into an unwavering standoff. For a split second, I saw her stare begin to soften and then she stood as if she were the neighborhood snitch.

Usually, I wouldn't care if a person knew my identity, but today was a little different.

I mean, walking into a nightclub on a Saturday night and getting noticed was nothing new; I had been doing that for years. But walking into God's house on Sunday and being noticed was something new.

I normally try to catch people before or after church, but what I was planning had taken balls, and I wanted to be there to witness it.

You're probably saying, "I thought I was safe from you in the house of God."

Nah! You're just fooling yourself!

People are convinced that just because they walk through the church doors on Sunday, I won't be there stoking those sinful desires and whispering in their ear.

"Look at Sister Jones! She thinks she's better than everybody. She thinks she's the shit just because she lives in a big house, drives a nice car, and her kids attend private school. Didn't you see her husband at the mall with his secretary? If I were you, I would tell Sister Evans about that. She has a knack for getting all the juicy rumors out."

No! I'm sorry. You are not safe from me! In fact, that's when I'm just getting started.

A part of me didn't care if the little girl pointed me out. But then again, I didn't want to get put out because I wanted to see how this played out.

I guess you're asking, "How do you put Satan out of the church?"

You ever heard that saying, "Resist the devil and he will flee?" Well, it's kind of true!

People seem to think that just because you throw the name of Jesus out there, I will leave you alone. Not true!

You might command me to leave you alone and I may just do so. But that's not saying I'm not coming back!

You can scream, "Get thee behind me Satan all day while you're in church." But I'll be waiting for you in the church parking lot doing pushups!

I'll let you in on a little secret! The best way to frustrate me and make me go away is to stay away from my friends and me and watch out for my schemes.

You say you want me to flee! You say you want to stomp on my neck! Well then, don't give me the opportunity to tempt you. If you see me or my allies coming your way, run and let God fight your battles. I never really understood why people like to get bold and fight me. I got way more resources, and the longer you spar with me, the stronger I get.

Frank had multiple opportunities to run, but I guess he thought he was stronger than me.

The little girl's name was Sarah. In Hebrew, the meaning of the name Sarah is: Princess. In the Bible, Sarah was the wife of Abraham and mother of Isaac. Her name was originally Sarai (quarrelsome), but God commanded that her name be changed to Sarah before the birth of her son.

Sarah had long, dark wavy hair, and a light brown complexion.

She stood for what seemed like an eternity as her stare was fixed directly on me. She finally turned toward Frank. She took a breath and began to sing, first under her breath as if to herself, and then loudly. Her voice was quavering and uncertain but still, she began to sing

"No weapon formed against me shall prosper, it won't work, No weapon formed against me shall prosper, it won't work, He will stand by His word, He will come through, Oh I won't be afraid of the arrows by day, From the hand of the enemy.

I can stand my ground with the Lord on my side. For the snares they have set will not succeed."

With each note, her voice got louder and stronger. Her voice was so pure, so rich, and filled with so much conviction. Her rendition of Fred Hammond's classic song was powerful.

Even though I knew she belonged to Christ, I truly was touched by her voice. Even a fallen angel could tell that God's hand was on this little girl.

The congregation began to stomp, and sway back and forth. It was like all the negative energy created by me was being extracted from the building, and it was being replaced by something warm and blissful.

Frank stood up and slowly began to walk towards the altar. He was sobbing loudly and begged God for forgiveness, and suddenly threw himself down on the floor.

He lay motionless face down and periodically his body would convulse, and he would murmur as if speaking in a different language.

I tried to regain control of the service through Fredrick. He stood up and tried to lead the choir to sing another song, but the Bishop silenced him.

Fredrick looked offended as he ran from the pulpit crying, but no one seemed to care. It was like everyone was oblivious to anything negative while Sarah was singing.

I could not believe what I was seeing! Fredrick is the boldest shit starter in the church when he's full of that Jezebel juice. And you mean to tell me that you couldn't switch a damn song selection.

Where are all my Jimmy's? Where are all my Tonya's? Where the hell are all my soldiers when I needed them most. A little girl had decimated my front-line infantry of Leeann and Fredrick, and now I was left to fend for myself.

Frank pulled himself up to his knees and started begging God for forgivingness, but I refused to give up without a fight. I sent a spirit flying at Frank with such velocity that it lunged him forward at least two feet.

But God is no punk! He wanted Frank to come back home. So, his body became a tug-of-war between two immortal powers. To the average human being, all you could see was Frank rolling back and forth on the floor begging God for strength. But it was more than that in the spiritual realm. It was a violent wrestling match for Frank's soul, and I was doing everything to keep him with me and make him turn his back on Christ.

I gave it my best shot, but Frank rejected my onslaught. He wanted God's spirit back in his life in the worst way, and he would not give up. He was like a cheating husband who realized he had made the worst mistake in the world. He was willing to do anything even if it meant death to get the love of his life back.

Suddenly, the church became completely silent, and Frank opened his eyes. He had a look of bewilderment on his face, but it was not a fearful look. He looked as though he was at peace.

I had seen the look many times over the centuries, but I will never forget the first time I saw it. The first time I saw such a content look in the face of war was during Christ's crucifixion.

When Christ screamed from the cross, "It is finished", I will never forget that look of joy and happiness, while surrounded by such chaos.

I damn near had his son begging me for mercy after dragging that three-hundred-pound cross through the street. Jesus' will to save mankind was impregnable, but he suffered greatly.

How would you feel staring death in the face? Your best friends sold you out and denied they ever knew you.

I had my most inhumane minions torturing Jesus for hours. My goal was to see Jesus die or save himself from a horrific death by using his powers. In either case, I would have won.

But Jesus endured, you should have seen the smile of victory as he took his last breath to save mankind.

Frank had that same smile across his face as he lay on the floor and lifted his hands to heaven and screamed, "Thank you, Lord, for forgiving me!"

It enraged me so much because I knew he had made it back over to the side of Christ.

Frank eventually was helped to his feet and Sarah handed him the microphone. He hugged her like she had just saved his life, and in a way, she.

Honestly, I didn't care if Frank lived or died. I just needed him to spread my message. He was a means to an end. Frank was a spell-binding orator, and hugely charismatic. He could mesmerize any audience, large or small, and he had exceptional people skills that could have taken him to even greater aspiration. His ability to analyze God's word and present it to anyone with authority was a gift.

I got chills just thinking about what he could have been for me. Frank standing in front of millions merging the word of God with my dogmas would have been extraordinary.

I had seen his father do it effortlessly, and he could have done the same.

Sarah looked at me with a triumphant gleam in her eyes, and all I could do was nod at her with my approval. She looked beautiful and regal as she slowly walked back to her seat, holding her father's hand. I couldn't help but respect what she had done, or should I say what God had done. What can I say! Sometimes God does his best work at the darkest and most difficult times.

Everyone was standing with their hands stretched toward the ceiling thanking God for Frank's deliverance.

All I could do was sit there feeling out of place while the congregation continued singing songs about deliverance. I felt like the lone black man at a Ku Klux Klan rally, and the Confederate Hymn was on repeat.

Everyone was looking at me while singing and uplifting Christ and they knew they were tormenting me. They were getting a kick out of pestering me, and there was absolutely nothing I could do.

I probably could have taken matters into my own hands and caused some type of disruption, but I been down that path before and I didn't like the outcome. God's unmistakable presence was slowly moving throughout the church, and I wanted no part of it.

I had experienced his presence several times in my life, the last being at a revival service in 1978. I tried to interfere with another prize prospect tarrying for the holy ghost at a small Pentecostal Church, in Danville KY. I was unceremoniously dismissed by God's spirit, in the form of a tacky dressing, light-skin Elder with an afro.

Again, I should have known something was out of place when I saw him stumbling around the pulpit and speaking in another language.

People were praying with this beautiful young lady at the altar, and I decided that I would take matters into my own hands.

I had tried every disruption in my arsenal aside from burning the church down, but nothing had worked. I was obstinate about keeping her on my team. She had more demons wrestling around in her than Mary Magdalene before she was saved. Now she was talking about getting the holy spirit. I told all my puppets to move aside and let me handle this. If you want shit done right, sometimes you have to do it yourself.

I walked to the front of the church and feigned as if I were praying. The crowd of people gathered around her parted just enough so that I could kneel beside her outstretched body.

I leaned forward and began to whisper in her ear.

"I know you're tired! You're doing all this praying for a gift, and no one's listening. You have to be honest with yourself; why would

God gift a sexually promiscuous whore like you with any type of Holy Spirit? Come on and get up! I know you're tired."

She tried to ignore me by keeping her eyes shut tight and crying out to God.

"Save me Jesus, fill me Jesus, "fill me with the Holy Ghost, come Jesus, hallelujah Jesus, sanctify me Lord, send your fire Lord."

I just kept whispering in her ear.

"He's not coming! Shut up! All those dicks that you sucked! Nah! Forget about it; he ain't coming by here, my Lord."

The older mothers in the church kept encouraging her by whispering in her other ear.

"Keep praying baby, let him have it, give it all to Jesus, give it up to God."

Other saints in the church also encouraged her by simply saying, "Hold on, sister! Don't give up."

This back and forth had been going on for hours, and then I saw this light-skinned man staggering towards me, mumbling with his eyes closed.

At first, I thought he was drunk. But as he got closer, I noticed that he was speaking to me in Latin.

" Ecce sto ad te in nomine Iesu Christi! Satanas, novi te intelligis. Ego sum Deus Abraham et Deus Isaac, et Jacob: et servo meo: non tangere. Satanas! Remove te a conspectu meo modo."

I paused and stood to my feet in amazement. I could not believe that this ordinary-looking man, wearing the cheap Woolworth's suit was addressing me by name in Latin.

Again, he called my name and pointed his finger directly at me.

His eyes were wide with confrontation as he repeated the previous statement, except this time it was in English.

"I rebuke you in the name of Jesus Christ. Satan, I know you understand me. I am the God of Abraham, Isaac, and Jacob, and you will not touch my servant. Satan! Remove yourself from my presence now."

I immediately moved back a couple of steps because it felt like the flesh that I was cloaked in was melting away. Every time I attempted to move forward I was stopped by the wild-eyed man in the cheap suit. Every fiber in me wanted to stay and fight for this soul, but I understood the power of God. I could only walk away in defeat that day, feeling like I had lost a great asset.

I started having similar feelings as soon as Frank began to give his testimony of deliverance.

Frank raised his hand and gave a loud, heavy sigh. I was surprised by his condition and thought he looked very well for what he had just been through. You just don't squabble with the devil and walk away like everything is good. Sometimes it takes every ounce of energy for a person to tarry their way back to Christ.

When I put a full court press on your soul, you better be able to withstand my assault, mentally, physically, and spiritually.

I had to give it to old Frank! He looked content, fulfilled, and exceedingly happy. A joyful smile danced across his face as he began his testimony. He began speaking slowly, carefully choosing his words and enunciating clearly.

"Saints of God, you will never know what I've been through this past couple of days!"

The congregation responded with a thunderous, "Amen."

"Saints, I was tempted by a spirit on Friday and instead of running away, I tried to fight it head-on. Saints, I want you to know that Satan and his minions are real."

I laughed to myself.

Minions?

Boy, what you got a hold of was some world-class pussy!

"You weren't sliding in and out of a minion! You were being held hostage by that thang, thang."

Frank's testimony gained momentum the longer he went on.

"I had always struggled with this person being in my life. But I had convinced myself that she was special to me. I saw all the warning signs, but I just didn't pay attention. Sometimes Satan positions obstacles in your life so that you can't break through. Sometimes you have to be smarter and go around or run in a different direction. I now understand what it means to let God fight my battles. I now understand that I don't have to be afraid or discouraged when bad things happen in my life. I don't have to feel alone and hopeless when I get overwhelmed by Satan's temptations. I now know that nothing is too beyond the scope of God's sovereign. In <u>Exodus 14:14,</u> Moses tells the children of Israel, "The Lord will fight for you; you need only to be still." The battle that I thought was mine was my God's all the time. God! Thank you for delivering me from backsliding. Today! The Lord has more than restored my walk with Him. My faith and my ministry have a new commitment to walk closer with God. Lord, God, I will never lose sight of you again."

The congregation erupted as Frank abruptly dropped the microphone and began to run around the church with his hands stretched toward the heavens screaming.

Thank you Lord, Hallelujah! Thank you Jesus, hallelujah!

I shook my head, aggravated that the music was encouraging him to run faster and faster.

I stood up to leave just as he was running near me. He must have thought that I was trying to give him a brotherly hug because he grabbed me like I was his long lost friend.

His body was warm but not overly warm. It was like a soft, vibrant glow that was very inviting, almost like the first warm spring day after winter.

The last time that I had this feeling was years ago when God had last hugged me. I wanted to push him away, but the warmth was so inviting and forgiving.

My momentary lapse for God's love quickly washed away when Frank whispered in my ear.

"Satan, I have been forgiven by God. I pray that God destroys you, and I pray for God to open my heart so that I will receive the love that will keep me from hurting your servants."

I was absolutely disgusted by what I heard, furious, and very much wanted him dead.

The nerve of this prick!

I couldn't believe that this person, who was just screwing my servant, now wanted me and her dead.

If God had not been protecting him at that moment, I would have brought him to his knees with grief.

"You think you're safe, don't you? The contract with God said I can't put my hands on you, Frank, not your crack headed ass cousin. Don't play games with me!"

I pulled away from Frank's embrace and quickly exited the church, humiliated once again by God.

I learned a very valuable lesson through Frank.

Sometimes, despite your best planning, you can fall victim to my temptations, but that does not mean you have to stay down.

Let me let you in on a little secret! I'm not going to stop tempting you, period! Even if you successfully fend off all of my enticements a hundred times straight, I'm coming back for number one hundred and one. And your defense better be strong enough to withstand my offenses, because I have every intention of capturing your soul.

Life as a Christian is like being in the army; it's an adventure. There are ups, downs, and unexpected turns. And sometimes you may even fall down on the treacherous trails, but you can't go backward.

Backsliding can carry devastating consequences. It can bring dishonor to you, your family, and most importantly, to your faith. The guilty feelings of despair or condemnation can be so powerful that some people never make it back to Christ.

If you take nothing else from this diary, always understand that you can always go back to God. Do not let anything hold you back from God's grace. And never let doubt and guilt keep you so miserable that you're afraid to ask God for guidance.

Frank!

Frank did well for himself. He continued to walk on the path of righteousness, and he was blessed with a God-fearing woman.

He eventually became Senior Pastor at St. Stephens. Frank also finally had that long talk with his father about the issues in the past, but he was more receptive to understanding his father's failures.

Frank had always had a hard time understanding how his parents could have been led astray so easily. He couldn't understand how the allure of money and power could replace Christ with deceit and betrayal.

Not doing or saying anything made Frank feel weak and spineless. And it truly affected his sense of self-worth. Whenever he and Edward came together during a visit, they argued. Frank felt like Edward should have been stronger when the family moved to Atlanta or sacrifice everything and move back to Cincinnati. But everything became ever-so-clear once he was placed in a similar circumstance.

Everybody thinks that they can be strong when Satan targets them with temptation, but I assure you that your attitude will change once I offer you everything that you've ever wished for.

 Mike Tyson said it best, "Everyone has a plan until they get hit!"

Now Frank understood the dilemma that his parents were presented with.

A blessing could have been anything when Edward was a working-class stiff, living paycheck to paycheck. Hell, he considered $5000 a miracle! But when you start bringing in $100,000 a week, your whole mindset changes.

Coming from a blue-collar background to millionaire status is intoxicating. Once Frank and Mariyah got a taste of success, they were instantly hooked. They become driven by their need for money – they loved it – they loved profits – they loved wealth and riches. They pursued what they loved, and they were willing to do anything to maintain that status, even if it meant compromising their faith.

This is when I can be so destructive to a family like the Barkley's. The offers and temptations presented to you surpass your wildest dreams. You start overlooking the small things and suddenly, you've lost your way.

It became easy for Edward to slide into a life of infidelity because everything else was being overlooked. It became easy to lie to the church members because the money and prestige masked them. Frank's mother became complicit because she covered Edward's wrongdoing. It was in Mariyah's best interest to keep quiet and enhance their income and reputation or risk losing everything.

As I stated before, I just present you with the choices, and you have to be the one that makes the situation.

As a teenager, Frank could not comprehend the intricate traps that I had laid for Frank's parents. Now, Frank had a deeper understanding of my capabilities and he forgave his father. And as a result, they became closer. But that's only because he worked through it with the encouragement of his mother. The smartest thing that Frank could have done was to forgive himself for the way he dealt with it.

He had to simply come to terms with the fact that Edward was not the paragon of morality and virtue when tempted. He was just a human being navigating his way through my strategically placed land mines. He had to let go of all the anger and contempt that he had for his father.

I enjoy it when you allow that hatred to build up and fester inside you. It's like a time bomb waiting to explode.

Leeann became that time bomb.

Don't get me wrong; she did well for herself!

She joined a sorority, graduated from college, and in most people's eyes, lived a comfortable life.

But she was toxic!

She never forgave herself for all the wrong she did, and it showed in her life. She was negative, selfish, delusional about herself, and jealous of others. If misery loves company, then Leeann was misery personified. She was still angry with her mother for not protecting her and it showed with her interactions. She never once considered that her inability to forgive was like drinking poison and hoping that it would kill the people who had hurt her.

As an adult, she was still stuck in that bedroom with Julius molesting her while her mother did nothing. And when her mother joined the church and hid behind her religion, it only infuriated her more. Her mother probably could have done a better job and apologized for not protecting her, but what good would it have done if Leeann was unwilling to forgive herself.

She enjoyed the company of miserable friends and she was attracted to miserable men. As a result, she was in and out of miserable relationships. She dated below her status to make herself feel better, but it only made her feel worse. A college graduate dating a high school dropout was not cute. But in her twisted mind, she was satisfied dating them. Those types of men were thrilled just to be in the same room with her and they placed her on a pedestal.

Dating men on or above her social status only complicated things, because of her Debbie Downer attitude. No one with anything positive going on in their lives wanted to deal with that much drama. Having to stroke her ego daily was a tough enough task.

She continued to seduce and deceive prophets and beloved religious leaders under my guidance because that's all she knew. She seduced spiritual leaders for sport, and the bigger the notoriety, the better she felt.

How did I repay her?

I killed her!

Well, actually her boyfriend killed her. He was driving her home after a night of partying and slammed his car into a telephone pole. He was never charged with the crime because he placed her dead body behind the wheel and told the first responders that she was driving.

How ironic! Live by deceit, die by deceit.

The lives of the Frank, Edward, Leeann, Tonya, and Jimmy are just small examples of how powerful I have become, and the deceptive snares I use to make you turn your back on Christ.

Eve, well that is a cautionary tale!

What would have happened if Eve would have said no to me?

Anyone can speculate! No death, no Satan, just a perfect relationship with God forever.

But I live in reality!

You must ask yourself, why would God create a perfect, immortal being, and place her in my realm? Command her not eat from one little tree without warning her about my snares. He had to know that I would never allow the main source of my humiliation to exist peacefully.

It's true, I was created to love God like his other creations, but over time my heart became cold. Imagine being in a situation when you were embarrassed and made to feel so low because of who you are. You did nothing wrong, and yet you are still forced to go through pain and humiliation. Wouldn't you want revenge?

My hatred towards God has no boundaries. He kicked the greatest asset in his kingdom to the side for a puny, sniveling, selfish, self-serving, disloyal, and unfaithful life form. When God turned his back on me, I never thought the pain and betrayal would be that significant, but it was. At that moment, I was convinced that God was the best thing that ever happened to me because I didn't know any better. Once I turned off my ability to see, understand, hear, and remember God, I became a machine! An unfeeling, uncaring, emotionless machine! When God kicked me out of heaven, I had to shut myself off to make life bearable. So, I don't love! I can't love! When I told God that I will put astray every human being and drag them to hell with me, I meant every word of it. Put it like this, anytime God's servants suffer, I'm incalculably satisfied. Although you have more knowledge, it's tarnished with elements from me: Distrustfulness, competitive, cynical, suspicious, sarcastic, prejudiced, and self-centered.

So, while you good saints of God are trying to figure out who can build the biggest church, I'm still up to my old tricks. Planning my next strategic move against the kingdom of God.

I guess you ask yourself why I keep fighting against God when I cannot possibly win? The answer is simple! If this were the Superbowl, it's the fourth quarter and I'm up by ten points. Translation, I've been doing a great job of controlling the game with my ground attack.

My team does a masterful job of tempting God's people, and it's apparent that they have a strong propensity to keep sinning. I notice that every day regardless of the situation, you think at least one sinful thought, speak one sinful word, or commit one sinful action.

Perhaps you should ask yourselves why you think you can get away with acting out of jealously, anger, greed, fear, pride, gluttony, laziness, and believe that you can defeat my kingdom!

All these qualities are the lifeline of my existence.

Understand, I'm not some cartoon with horns and a red cape, plotting your demise somewhere in the pits of hell.

I'm right beside you every day, whispering to your little fragile self-esteem.

Nobody sees themselves fighting against God, especially the bible thumpers. But you all do it every single day, whether you are aware of it or not. Half of your actions and thoughts are generated by jealousy alone! You want the fancy car like your neighbor, the respect that Jay-Z and Beyoncé have, the perfect relationship like the Obamas.

Where is God in that little equation?

Why so many churches, beliefs, and spiritual leaders! What prevents you from being a spiritual army united against me?

Let me answer that question for you!

2000 plus years of division, distrust, jealousy, arrogance, and self-interest keep you divided among yourself.

Well! Good luck walking that righteous path! I'll keep making offers, and you keep trying to resist me. Just remember, I know your heart, and I have everything you desire.

Satan!

Steven Darrell Bates Sr. is from Cincinnati, Ohio and attended the University of Cincinnati where he earned a degree in Criminal Justice. In 2004, he moved to Atlanta, Georgia to continue his career working with At-Risk Youth.

Being raised in the Pentecostal Holiness church and by a minister, he was on a strict regimen of religious beliefs. He was not allowed to watch TV, play cards, attend movie theaters, or listen to secular music. This lead Steve to gravitate towards reading and writing just as long as it was not church related. He always felt like he was held to a higher standard because his father was a minister and the beliefs placed on him by the church. While growing up, Steven was expected to become a minister but that was a frightening thought for him. As a young man, he had to stop living up to other people's expectations, and start living his own life.

Later in life, Steven Darrell Bates's artistic talents surfaced, inspiring him to become a writer. He writes to admit to himself that he can create a story where the church and the secular society come together. While in college, he developed a deep fascination for understanding the church, GOD, and the concept of spirituality.

While many of those thoughts still elude him, he was lucky enough to find his one true love, his wife, and he is living happily ever after with her and their two kids. He is currently working on his third book.

Visit Steven's website @ www.stevendarrellbates.com